I0721355

CHRISTINE A. SCHIMPF

Catching a Cowboy

Christine A. Schimpf

ISBN-13: 978-1-959788-84-3

In loving memory of my dad,
Robert *Peanuts* Wagner
Who taught me what it felt like to be loved

Faith Statement
Joshua 1:9 *Have I not commanded you? Be strong and courageous. Do not be frightened, and do not be dismayed, for the Lord your God is with you wherever you go.* (ESV)

Chapter 1

Twenty-five-year-old Cassie Hamilton was in the hot seat.

"You have two choices." Brett Hayward's gaze was serious. He leaned back in his chair and steepled his fingers.

Cassie felt the weight of her accountant's look as if she'd strapped a fifty-pound sack of baker's flour onto her back. Seated across from him in his office, she shifted her eyes around the minimalistic designed room, wishing she'd canceled their quarterly meeting.

"You'll need to find a way to bring in revenue over the off-season or build up sales during your peak periods."

Cassie sighed. With the tourist season winding down, she had no idea how she'd manage that.

"If you continue to draw from your funds to keep the café going, you'll end up running your savings into the ground."

Cassie was guilty of sticking her hand into the cookie jar far too often this past year. Watching her savings account dwindle was painful. She never expected it would be this hard. "I understand."

The old-school grandfather clock that stood in the corner of the room ticked off another minute, inching time toward the dreaded down season. Cassie pulled a spiral notebook and ballpoint pen from her satchel ready to take notes on the solution to her problem.

Mr. Hayward swiveled his computer in her direction. A sea of numbers in an Excel file glared back at her. "As you know, many of the businesses here in Door County operate on a seasonal basis. They close their doors over the winter months for good reason."

Yes, Cassie knew the stats but didn't believe the café would struggle. She leaned on her headstrong attitude and opened up the Perfect Cup café last December. She hoped her establishment would be a welcomed addition, especially for the tourists coming into the county to enjoy the brand-new sledding hill and winter activities.

"I promised your parents to oversee your first year by reviewing your books every three months. I'm sorry to have to deliver such a strong message."

Cassie stopped the repetitive click of the ballpoint pen when Mr. Hayward's eyes drifted to her hand. She placed the pen on the desk. "I agree with you. I can't keep dipping into my savings." This meeting was beginning to sound like a broken record.

Mr. Hayward's eyes softened. "I understand. You love your café, but I'm sure you don't want to operate at a loss."

Cassie grabbed the pen ready to put it to work. She

peered up at the man seated across from her. "I'm open to suggestions, but every small business endures the pinch during winter."

Mr. Hayward released a heavy sigh.

Cassie fumed. Why couldn't she experience the same good fortune as her parents had with their fishing excursion business or her brother, Conrad's, success with Hamilton Construction? Both had lucrative, thriving businesses. Born into a family of entrepreneurs, she'd be the only Hamilton who wouldn't be a success in three generations if her café failed. She couldn't let that happen. Even her grandparents found luck with their rental cottages. She needed some lucrative suggestions and fast. She hoped Mr. Hayward could point her in the right direction.

Instead, he shook his head, causing his full cheeks to wobble. "I don't know what to tell you, but I'd advise you to stay open-minded. Have you heard the county is holding the Rising Star competition again? That may open some doors to new opportunities for you. Even as a contestant, the café could garner some exposure, leading to more sales opportunities."

Cassie repositioned herself in the chair. "A committee stopped by the café a couple of weeks ago. I told them I wasn't interested."

"Why not? Your café is perfect."

"I haven't had the time to think it through. I've been training a part-time waitress to help me during rush hour. Customers were walking out the door because I couldn't get to them."

"I strongly urge you to contact that committee and sign up."

"But if the judges discover that my sales plummet

in the off-season, how much of a rising star business do I have?"

Mr. Hayward rolled up his sleeves as if the next order of business was to help her solve the biggest problem of her life. "Your family has had successful businesses in the county for generations. Why don't you ask them for a little support?"

Cassie didn't want to do that. She was certain they'd agree to help her, but it was time she stood on her own two feet, both personally and professionally. "I'd rather figure this out on my own. Please don't mention anything to my dad." Mr. Hayward was an avid fisherman and regularly frequented her parent's bait shop.

The accountant straightened the edges of a stack of manilla folders on his desk and then glanced at the clock. "No need to worry. We have a confidentiality agreement here, similar to the one you'd have with an attorney. You'll come up with a solution. You Hamiltons always do."

Cassie thanked him for his time and left the office for the short walk back to the diner. She digested the conversation as she crossed the street, kicking the fallen cinnamon-colored leaves and acorns out of her path. The heady scent of the changing season filled the air. Autumn had always been an energizing time of the year for her, but the meeting had her spirits dragging. She loved living in Wisconsin and especially in her hometown of Sister Bay but running her own business was a lot more than she bargained for. She watched the first glimmer of light from the morning sun and paused her stride, then closed her eyes. *Good morning, Lord, looks like we have a problem to figure out.* After a moment, she walked up to her yellow clapboard building trimmed out in white and topped off with a green tin roof. She unlocked the door and stepped into the kitchen through the back door.

"Hey, Ruby, girl," Cassie greeted her sleepy golden lab mix snuggled in her basket in the crate and then clicked on the coffee roasters. After slipping an apron over her head and securing it behind her waist, she prepared for the day. She wrote the words pumpkin spice on a white-washed chalkboard she used to announce the daily specials. She hoped the social media posting she did last night would result in a good crowd today.

An hour later, she was thrilled with a full house. If only the meeting with Mr. Hayward would stop percolating in her head. Cassie scanned the nearly packed room, loving what she saw and wishing it could be this good all year round. The financial pickle she was in was serious, and if she didn't succeed, Conrad would tease her forever. She couldn't let that happen. Maybe she should consider the competition.

As morning inched toward noon, if not for the bell over the door that chimed, Cassie wouldn't have noticed another customer had arrived. She shot a quick look in the newcomer's direction, noticed the cowboy hat on his head, then focused on refilling two cups of coffee for the McPhersons who sat at their favorite corner table.

The newly arrived headed straight for the jukebox. Soon, country music filled the café but the pleasant moment didn't last long. Cassie spotted Ruby bolting from the kitchen toward the opened entrance door. Coffee pot in hand, Cassie quick-stepped toward her.

Why hadn't she latched the crate? Oh, right. Because Ruby had been snoozing peacefully just twenty minutes ago.

"Whoa there, little girl." Mr. Good Looking wrapped his large hands around Ruby's middle, stopping her determined route toward freedom. "You remind me of my dog, Blazer, back home."

The voice sounded familiar, but Cassie couldn't quite place the name. She took in the details of the man in front of her. His gentle touch settled Ruby to roll over. The pup offered up her belly for a rub.

"She was sound asleep not too long ago." Why was she stammering in front of this total stranger? *Wait a minute.* "Is this who I think it is under that cowboy hat?"

"In the flesh." Luke Hunter lifted the hat from his head, revealing an unruly head of sandy-brown hair.

Cassie spotted the scar over his left eyebrow. The accident that caused the mark happened so long ago. Luke had pushed her out of the way of an oncoming wooden swing but wasn't quick enough to save himself from the hit. Now, the same grey-blue eyes lifted and met hers.

Cassie took in his strong arms beneath a cotton plaid shirt, the indigo jeans covering his long legs straight down to the camel-colored boots on his feet. The years had seasoned him into a handsome man and the cowboy hat added to his good looks. By the looks of him, he must've turned country after his family moved to Nashville. *But what is he doing here?*

"Meeting your brother, Conrad." He tipped his head toward her, wearing a grin.

Her smile shifted to a frown. "I didn't ask the

question yet." The prickle of perspiration dotted her forehead. Why hadn't Conrad warned her that he was meeting Luke today? At the minimum, she could have glossed her lips over with a little color.

Luke lifted two fingers. "Yeah, you did. I saw the question in those double browns of yours."

Double browns! Cassie rolled her eyes at the old nickname Conrad had given her because of her almond-shaped brown eyes. And if Conrad used it, his pals did too.

"No one's called me that in more than a decade." She wanted to rid herself of the childish nickname she'd carried far too long.

"Still true." Luke rolled Ruby to her feet and drew her close. He looked her over with his veterinary eyes and then squinted at Cassie. "She's not getting a walk every day, is she?"

Cassie shook her head. She was usually one step ahead of most people. *How could he have known that?* "I...."

Luke slid his hands down the dog's belly and legs. "Has she had her one-year-old wellness checkup yet?"

Cassie didn't have to check the calendar on her phone to answer Luke's question. Ruby's appointments were on a sticky note on her fridge. "Her appointment is next week."

"Good. I'm taking over all new patients at Happy Paws for Uncle Russ until the clinic sells. I'll be seeing you both then."

The clinic sells? Cassie knew Doc Hunter wanted to retire but selling the clinic? Is that why Luke came back? Cassie bristled at the idea of a total stranger in charge of Ruby's care or having to drive down to

Sturgeon Bay for Ruby's vet visits. She had come to rely on the gentle, holistic approach she received at Happy Paws and didn't want one of those cookie-cutter franchises to move in. Before she could investigate and ask the question, Luke beat her to it with his own.

"Where would you like me to deposit your little princess?"

"Ruby," Cassie corrected. With the sound of her mistress's voice, the dog's tail began a frantic swish. "Has a crate in the kitchen, but I don't expect you to …."

Though a few inches taller than her five-foot-seven-inch frame, he'd filled out. Gone was the lanky young man of his youth, and in his place, stood a physically fit, strong adult with broad shoulders and strong hands. With the pup cradled under his arm, Luke stepped around the counter and strode into the kitchen as if he'd walked the path a hundred times before.

Chapter 2

The first truth that hit Luke square in the chest after he walked into the kitchen, was how beautifully Cassie Hamilton had grown up, and how she hadn't lost her feisty attitude. *Good.* She'd grown taller since he'd seen her last and imagined how she'd stand out in a crowd. He grinned at having remembered her nickname. Conrad had given it to her to discourage her from hanging around the guys.

Luke hadn't doubted Cassie would turn out to be a beauty. He saw that coming even when she was a skinny, little pipsqueak of a girl, standing in Conrad's shadow. Back then, she'd worn her hair tied in a ponytail high on her head. Now, her thick locks boasted the color of rich chocolate with streaks of coppery red from the summer sun.

He thought plenty about dating her. *Out of the question.* Cut from the same cloth as his father, Luke was a rolling stone, moving from job to job. That would never do for a family like hers.

Luke ruffled the soft spot behind the pup's ears, thinking of his own dog, Blazer, back home. He hoped it wouldn't be too long before he'd get settled in his new job and send for him. He deposited Ruby into the crate and secured the lock. He scanned the kitchen and found an industrial double sink, a coffee roaster perking fresh brews, and an electric vac in the corner. He spotted the dirty cups that needed a wash and wished he had the time to help.

Cassie peeked around the corner. "Conrad's here."

"Right behind you." Walking back into the dining area, Luke spotted Conrad squeezing the shoulders of someone seated at the counter. Probably razing the poor guy. Conrad was good at that. Luke walked in his direction.

He laid a hand on Conrad's back and then stuck out his hand when his friend turned to face him. "Good to see you, brother," he said, realizing how much he'd missed his old buddy.

Conrad returned a strong handshake. "Too long, my friend. Let's grab a seat."

Cassie motioned them to a table and Conrad gave her the peace sign—the silent language for two cups of coffee.

"How's business?" Luke asked while keeping tabs on Cassie. She moved with butterfly agility around them. *Impressive.* Luke wanted to ask Conrad how her business was doing but then remembered how protective he always was over her.

"Screamin'," Conrad answered, steering Luke's attention away from his little sister. "Building a lot of four-season additions."

It didn't surprise Luke to hear that Conrad's business took off with his family roots sewn deep in the county. "Uncle Russ has told me a million times, 'When business is good life is good.'"

"He's right. People are sticking their hard-earned

dollars into renovations. It sure beats selling and moving."

Luke silently disagreed since he'd adopted his parents' view on life. With a job-jumper for a dad, Luke had grown used to what his parents called 'the next great adventure'. He leaned back into his chair, content to listen to Conrad and all that he'd accomplished. "By the way, congrats on the baby. A son, right?"

Conrad's face broke out in a wide smile. "Thank you. We're loving every minute of it."

"It's good you've got a booming business. Kids can be expensive."

Conrad chuckled, giving Luke the assumption that he wasn't concerned. "Thanks. We're head-over-heels for the little guy. Lila wanted to name him after her dad."

Luke threw him a puzzled look. He couldn't remember Lila's father's name.

Conrad leaned in. "Robert. We call him Bobby for short. Sometimes, Bobbo. Cute as all get out." He pulled out his wallet from a back pocket to retrieve a cascade of photos. "Even though Bobby will never get the chance to meet Lila's dad, he'll carry his namesake. It was important to her, and I was good with it. The firstborn grandson comes with a bit of a tradition in her family."

Luke raised his hands. "Hey, I love tradition. It's one of the reasons I enjoyed coming up here every summer after we moved to Nashville. There always seemed to be some kind of annual festival going on or a birthday party that needed to be celebrated at the town hall. The best part was, everyone was invited, including me."

Conrad shot him a blank stare. "Why wouldn't you be invited?"

Luke scoffed. Conrad didn't get the nomadic lifestyle he lived with his parents. Where uprooting the family every few years was the norm like it always had been for him. Finding a place where you put down roots and belonged was never a priority in the home he grew up in. He could count on one hand how many celebrations he'd attended like birthday parties and weddings.

Conrad's face lit up. "Speaking of parties, we're giving the little guy a first birthday bash next week. Our place. Consider yourself officially invited."

Luke wasn't surprised, though he didn't have a clue where to find a gift.

Cassie breezed by and filled their cups with hot coffee. Ruby followed close behind her. *Adorable.*

Cassie's cheeks took on the flush of a woman in charge of her establishment. She could have easily passed for a model for a Door County vacation advertisement. Luke continued to watch her as she filled cups, doled out pastries, and returned dirty dishes to the kitchen, all while wearing a smile.

As Cassie fluttered from table to table, Luke overheard some of her comments. She talked of last night's full moon or how delicious the sweet corn had been this year. She was connected to the community in a way he'd never been and never would be. Not with the plans he had set in place. He'd been groomed as a kid to keep moving to take advantage of everything the world had to offer him. His parent's philosophy on life was now his.

Conrad's face turned serious. "Let's hear it. With

that vet degree in your back pocket, tell me your plans."

Luke sensed Conrad's anticipation in the grin he wore on his face. "This might surprise you, but I'm moving toward a final interview with PetsAmerica." A nervous laugh escaped him, as he tried to guess how Conrad would take his news.

Conrad's mouth gaped. "That big-dog franchise that has clinics across the country?" His shoulders hit the back of the wooden chair, causing a groan.

"That's the one." Luke was well aware of what his friend and the rest of the community expected of him— to take over his Uncle Russ's vet practice when he retired. He wouldn't enjoy setting everyone straight in this part of the visit.

Conrad thumbed over his shoulder in the direction of Happy Paws Clinic right down the road. "And your Uncle Russ's place? We all assumed you'd take over."

Just as I thought. Luke blew out a breath.

"Wasn't that the plan from the get-go and why you came up here every summer?"

Luke had trouble remembering when the idea to take over the clinic began. "It might have been at one time, but if I get in with Pets, I can live in all fifty states by transferring to another location every three years. That includes Puerto Rico." The job would fit his lifestyle perfectly.

Conrad grew uncharacteristically silent, leaving Luke with the notion that he'd broken some sort of unspoken promise. His parents had loved the idea when he'd told them about the opportunity and his Uncle Russ, although disappointed, said he'd understood. But it was clear Conrad was having none of it. That meant no one else would either. The mountain of opposition grew.

Conrad poured himself another cup of coffee from the carafe, offered one to Luke, then asked for the small decanter of cream. "Technically, Puerto Rico isn't a state. And what do you mean every three years?"

Luke's spirits lifted. If Conrad was asking questions, maybe he was beginning to see Luke's point. Luke squared up his shoulders. "The company offers their vets a three-year contract. At the end of the term, I have the option to relocate to any one of their locations across the country. I could live in Alaska if I wanted to."

Luke's optimism was short-lived when Conrad winced. "Alaska? What do you want up there? Lila and I took a cruise there last year. We couldn't wait to get back home. If you're looking for cold weather, we've got enough for you right here."

Luke's frustration mounted. "It's not the same and you know it. Imagine, over the next twenty years, I could live in a half-dozen different places. It's an unbelievable opportunity."

Conrad shrugged a shoulder. "If you say so, but it's not what I expected to hear from you today. Not sure how that'll go down around here. You're going to disappoint a lot of people." Conrad scanned the room as if taking a mental count against Luke's idea and then motioned Cassie over. "Did you hear his plans?"

Cassie held a large tray of delectable sweets including cherry scones and blueberry muffins. She placed a small platter of each in the center of their table. She gave Luke a questioning gaze. "I thought I heard him mention something about selling the clinic. Tell me it's not true."

Luke's body tensed. A big heap of unearned shame spread from his gut to his toes.

Cassie's eyes softened. "You know how the folks are up here. Their pets are part of their family, as close as a son or daughter. They trust your Uncle Russ at Happy Paws. That trust isn't given easily. Now that I have Ruby, I'm concerned about her care and who will be her vet."

Luke couldn't put a finger on it, but Cassie's reaction bothered him, even more than Conrad's opposition. Usually, Luke sprinted ahead in life with his plans, not giving opinions from others much credence. Today was different. His heart picked up beats with the door chime. It sent Cassie back on duty with her customers, but she took with her a look of disappointment.

That he caused.

Luke downed half a cup of his coffee. This was going to be harder than he ever imagined. He shifted his gaze back to Conrad. "I'll be here for the short term. Uncle Russ has a mess at the clinic. I told him I'd help him out with everything, including the sale and the transition of power to the new owner."

"He told Lila as much when she took Chester in for his appointment. Said he's overwhelmed and doesn't have the oomph for a full day of patients anymore. And that arthritis of his." Conrad shook his head. "Lila had to help him out during Chester's visit." Conrad finished the rest of his coffee and then chose one of the cherry scones.

Luke's mouth gaped. "Wait a minute. Chester? You and Lila have a pet?"

Conrad's face lit up like that of a much younger

man. "Yup. Big black lab mix. Got him through the adoption event at Happy Paws."

Luke's shoulders hit the back of his chair. "My uncle is still running that, too?" Luke had encouraged him to give that up years ago. It sounded as if his advice was never taken.

When Conrad grinned, Luke added another item to the mental to-do list for the clinic. "Let me get this straight. You got married, adopted a dog, and had a baby, all within a year. I've got a dog too, but all of this is hard to believe."

Conrad finished the scone in three bites then eased back in his chair. His arms folded across his chest. "Don't forget about the cabin," he said, smacking his lips clean of vanilla icing.

"You finished the house, too? Man, I hope I don't catch whatever you got. You're trapped here forever."

Conrad lifted a brow. "Trapped? There's no place I'd rather be, and no one else I'd rather be with than Lila and Bobbo. I hope you find that, too, one day."

Luke never wanted anything more than his vet license and his dog, Blazer, in the back seat of his Jeep. He gave his friend a measured look. *He's dead serious.*

"You sticking around for Chet's wedding?"

"Wouldn't miss it." He had to decline to attend Conrad and Lila's wedding because of the veterinarian licensing exam. He didn't intend on missing Chet's. Luke was looking forward to seeing another good friend. "I don't want to miss Chet Taylor going down. Plan to rub his nose in his own words."

"What do you mean?" Conrad shot him a questioning look.

Luke glanced around before speaking. He didn't

want those within earshot to hear a word. "Remember how he bragged? His exact words were, he'd be the last man to fall."

Conrad chuckled. Both men knew that Chet had broken enough hearts to fill up the back end of a pickup truck. That was until Andrea Lockhart walked into his life at Conrad and Lila's wedding last year.

Conrad gave his familiar fist pump. "That's right. He gave me some grief on my wedding day. Looks like the last man standing is now you."

Luke grinned, enjoying the pride that filled him for having claimed the title. He was confident in the plans he'd set for his life even if they didn't include getting married.

"You bringing a date?"

Luke scanned the room for Cassie. *Where is she?* "Solo. Just the way I like it."

Conrad motioned Cassie over to their table. "Cass, do you have a date yet for Chet and Andrea's wedding?"

Luke noticed the blush on Cassie's cheeks. Couldn't Conrad have been more discreet? He ignored the onlookers who waited for her answer.

To Luke's surprise, Cassie didn't back down. She probably had tough skin after years of living with a big, older brother.

"Not yet, why?" she asked.

"Luke here is going solo. He's the only man I'd trust as your date." Conrad shot Cassie a quick wink.

Cassie rolled her eyes. "Really, Conrad? I don't need you to navigate the waters of my dating life anymore. It was cute when I was younger, but enough already. I'm twenty-five years old."

Luke lifted a shoulder. "Hey, I don't mind if you don't." When Luke saw the dramatic change in Cassie's face, he wished he would've chosen his words more carefully.

Cassie turned to him, eyes blazing, hands on her hips.

By the looks of her, Luke could probably use a lesson in discretion, right along with Conrad. He stiffened.

"Oh, you wouldn't, would you? It sounds as if I should be grateful. Okay, big guy, you're on. But you're not my date, you're my plus-one. Big difference."

Luke steered his next question in Conrad's direction. "What's a plus-one?"

Conrad released a hearty laugh. "Don't ask me. I've been off the market for years."

Cassie bent at the waist, inching toward Luke. The sweet fragrance of lilac hit him straight on. "A plus-one means friends only."

Luke looked from Conrad into Cassie's chocolate browns. "Ah, right."

Conrad interrupted the moment. "By the way, you two may want to get up to speed on the dance floor. There's a competition at the wedding. I'll make sure you get on the list of contestants."

Luke shook his head. The invitation he received didn't mention a competition. The whole idea sounded a bit off to him. Conrad must've heard wrong.

"A competition?" Cassie asked. It sounded as if she was as much in the dark as he was.

"Chet said he and Andrea wanted to spice things up at the wedding with a dance competition for the guests. If you win, you get dinner on them at an undisclosed location. Chet gave me the heads-up because I've got two left feet on the dance floor. Lila and I have been practicing in the kitchen at night. Bobby gets a kick out of watching us."

"Adorable." Cassie shook her head and sent copper strands of hair to drape across her neck. "I can just see him watching Mommy and Daddy dance. I love competitions."

"Besides being married to your job you mean?" her brother asked.

Cassie ignored Conrad's question, but it popped one into Luke's mind. *Why is someone as special as Cassie still single?*

Cassie's gaze turned to Luke. "Can you dance?"

Luke hesitated. He'd managed to get himself invited to a one-year-old's birthday party, a date for the wedding, and had entered a dance competition all under five minutes. He sucked in a mouthful of air buying himself some time. "I can manage a country two-step. But I'm going to need something from you in return."

Cassie's eyebrows lifted, revealing specks of gold in her eyes Luke hadn't seen before.

"Like what?"

"Picking out a baby present."

Cassie flashed Luke a quick wink. "We got this," she said and gave him a smile that made him glad he was sitting down.

Chapter 3

First thing Monday morning, Luke surveyed the crowded parking lot at the Happy Paws Clinic. *What's going on?* He searched for the *Physicians Only* spots. No luck, most likely ignored by someone with an emergency. He had no alternative but to park on the street. He'd have to move his vehicle later and avoid a parking ticket. Right now, he'd better get inside.

He spotted Uncle Russ cradling the phone in the crook of his neck and rubbing his arthritic hands together—a tell-tale sign that the stress of the morning was getting the best of him. Relief flooded his uncle's face when their eyes locked until the caller pulled him back to the conversation. A line of impatient pet owners waited to be checked in. A soft growl pulled Luke's attention to the waiting area. He grinned at an aged retriever tolerating a French bulldog puppy's antics with limited patience.

"Luke, it's good to see you." His uncle hung up the phone. He gave Luke a nod to follow him to one of the examining rooms.

Luke grabbed a white lab coat from the rack and slipped it on while he followed his uncle down the hall. "What is going on here?" He did his best to camouflage the look of concern that must've been on his face.

His uncle shook his head sending his salt-and-pepper hair askew. Luke noticed he was wearing two different colored socks—one blue and one black. He was probably running late again this morning.

"Just doing my best to make ends meet."

"It's barely eight a.m. Are you opening earlier than you used to?" For years the clinic operated under a nine-to-five schedule with Fridays closing early at two-thirty.

Spraying down the examining table with a disinfectant, Uncle Russ pulled a cleaning cloth from a back pocket and began wiping down the surface. "You bet I am. They start coming in as early as seven-thirty some days. It's the only way I can fit them all in."

"What happened to BettyAnn and the appointment schedule?"

"BettyAnn?" Uncle Russ waited as if Luke would fill in the missing blank. Had he forgotten his 40-plus-year office assistant?

"Retired last year. I never could figure out how she ran the office end of things. I should've retired when she did and taken Cathy up on her offer to head south, but I waited for you to finish your schooling."

"Cathy?"

"It doesn't matter now. All that has changed." Uncle Russ plopped himself into one of the orange plastic chairs he'd purchased when he opened the place more than forty years ago.

The screws of Luke's decision tightened. His uncle's spirits had a way of snowballing. He'd better move this conversation into positive territory. "It'll all be over soon now that you found a buyer. What time are you expecting them today?"

Uncle Russ rose and turned toward the small sink in the room. He gingerly pumped the soap dispenser more times than needed. "Yes… about that. I've got some bad news on that front." He tore off a sheet of paper toweling and worked it around his swollen knuckles, wincing as much as drying his hands. "They pulled out after the tour. Said they didn't want to rebuild the place from the ground up."

His words hit Luke in the gut like a fist from a prize fighter. "You've got to be kidding. What's wrong with the place?" He could've listed a half-dozen things in the short five minutes he'd been standing in the building, but he wanted to hear it from the buyer's perspective.

Uncle Russ shook his head. "I don't understand it either. They talked about streamlining services and outsourcing. According to them, even the building needs renovation—both inside and out. I don't know what they're talking about. I figured you could do a better job with it all."

"Me?" Luke barked back louder than he would have liked. "I can't handle anything. I've got an interview set with PetsAmerica right after Chet's wedding." *This is exactly what I didn't want to get stuck doing.*

"Don't worry about them. They dole out interviews like we do dog biscuits for good behavior."

Luke couldn't deny that. The interview came pretty easily. He turned his attention from his uncle to the academic plaques that hung on the wall above the fishing trophy rack. Despite his busy practice, Uncle Russ had always set aside time to enjoy his life. In the years Luke had worked with him over the summers, he'd taught him a gentle approach to animals and introduced a holistic path of service, but he also instilled a love for the outdoors and a passion for horseback riding.

He owed him.

The counter bell rang out a repetitive jingle, reminding them of the waiting area full of pets and their owners. Luke bit the side of his cheek, placed the stethoscope around his neck, and followed his uncle down the hall. He didn't expect to have to call and reschedule the final interview. Now he'd have to. The place needed some work if he was going to be the one responsible for getting it sold. And that's how it sounded as of right now.

He walked past the chalkboard and read the names scribbled down for the day's appointments. Cassie and Ruby were expected later in the afternoon. *Good.* Luke plastered a smile on his face and then walked into the waiting room to face the mayhem. "Okay, who's next?"

~

Later that afternoon, Cassie hustled through the parking lot of Happy Paws Vet Clinic tugging Ruby behind her. Ruby's normal demeanor—bouncy and happy-go-lucky had disappeared overnight. She began showing signs of distress right after supper. Cassie blamed herself for having to reschedule her wellness check. Having a puppy to snuggle up with at night was one of the benefits she enjoyed, but she was guilty of not following through on all of the responsibilities of owning a pet. Bracing herself for another stern lecture from Luke, Cassie opened the door to the clinic and stepped inside.

"Right on time," Luke said from behind the registration counter. "You can bring her right back."

"Looks like they're having fun," Cassie motioned at a pair of black lab puppies tangling up their leashes while the owner tried her best to keep them apart. Luke chuckled and Cassie followed him to a large scale to take Ruby's weight and measure her height.

Luke ruffled Ruby's ear. "You are one of my favorite breeds, little girl. You've got more golden in you than Labrador by the looks of you." He noted her weight and height on a chart and then directed Ruby and Cassie to an examining room. "How's your little princess doing?"

Cassie placed the leash and her purse on a chair. *Here it goes.* "I'm not sure. She's lethargic and has low energy. And her appetite is off. I'm concerned."

Luke placed Ruby on the stainless steel table and pressed the stethoscope against her chest. Using two fingers of both hands, he pressed gingerly on one side of her stomach and then the other. After taking her temperature, he examined her ears, eyes, nose and teeth, providing Cassie with nothing more than a nod and an mm-hmm as if she could read his mind.

Cassie had trouble waiting for Luke's assessment. She surveyed the room, trying to sidetrack her impatience. Her eyes landed on the dog breed chart that hung on the wall. If she was at fault, she wished he'd just come out and say it. Knowing Luke, he was probably crafting the message to lessen the sting. "So, what is it?"

"Other than what you've told me, her vitals, weight, and height are good. Her teeth and gums are excellent, and so are her eyes. She is running a low-grade fever. I'd like to hold off on giving her any vaccinations today. It means another visit, but I think it's a wise approach."

Cassie had to ask the question. "Is it my fault for not bringing her in on time?"

Luke tilted his head. "Although I wouldn't recommend postponing wellness checks, I don't think you're to blame here. Is it possible she got into something? Maybe ate something she shouldn't have?"

It hit her like a new coffee blend she wanted to add to the menu. "I know this might sound gross, but she thinks the bird bath is her water dish. I scolded her last week after she emptied nearly half of it."

Luke chuckled. It was a nice laugh, low and rumbly, soothing to Cassie's ears.

"Bingo. I suspect a bacterial infection. Let me take some blood to confirm it but an antibiotic should clear it up in a few days." He pulled a syringe from a drawer and prepared to take the blood sample.

Luke bent at the waist to peer eye-to-eye with Ruby. "You'll be feeling better real soon, sweet girl." He'd entered Ruby's territory where she'd freely plastered kisses if given the chance. Luke didn't budge or pull back; instead, he accepted a face full of wet thank-yous.

It was obvious he'd adopted the same gentle approach with animals as his Uncle Russ had with his canine patients.

"Give her a couple of weeks before bringing her in for the vaccinations. Other than that, she's in perfect health."

"Great, thanks so much." Cassie grabbed her purse and leash from the chair. "Was this your first full day?"

She clipped the leash onto Ruby's collar.

Luke opened the examining room door. "Yup."

Now she was curious. "How did it go?"

He walked down the hall in the direction of the red exit sign.

Cassie recognized the empty examining rooms. She was probably the last appointment of the day.

"Let's just say, not what I expected."

This didn't sound good. She hoped he wasn't intending to leave before the clinic sold. That wouldn't be the Luke she had come to know over the years. Typically, he gravitated toward the underdogs in life with a helping hand or advice. "Oh, no. Sounds serious."

Luke spoke over his shoulder in a whisper. "The sale on the clinic fell through for Uncle Russ. Looks like I'll be sticking around for a while. I'll need to implement some changes and beef up the place if I want to attract buyers. I hope to give it a major facelift so it ends up in a bidding war for the place. I've already touched base with a commercial realtor."

Cassie smiled, not because the sale had fallen through, or the idea of a bidding war, or that he'd contacted a realtor already, but what she heard between the lines. Luke hadn't changed over the years. He'd see this through for his uncle for as long as it would take. "What about your interview with PetsAmerica?"

"At this point, I'll have to reschedule."

"Oh-oh. That doesn't sound good."

Luke shook his head. "I can only hope they understand, but I've got to stick around and help Uncle Russ. He's done a lot for me."

"You mean all the years he let you work at the

clinic?"

Luke slid Ruby's chart in front of a deep line of others in a plastic bin marked *Today's Patients*. "Not only that but for all the encouragement and advice he gave me throughout school and during my internship. He's the one who encouraged me to get a job at the racehorse ranch before I started coming back here in the summers."

"You always were conscientious growing up. It doesn't surprise me you're still thinking of others first now."

He peered up at her.

That's when it hit her. *Those eyes of his will do me in one day.*

"You give me more credit than I deserve."

Cassie disagreed. He wouldn't bail, even though it meant he'd lose out on what he believed was the opportunity of a lifetime. She wasn't sure how easy it was for him to land that interview, but she knew canceling it was not a good idea.

"Are we still on for baby gift shopping on Friday?" she asked.

"You bet. We close early on Fridays. Text me when you're ready. I'd like to get a quick horseback ride in before picking you up."

"No kidding? Where did you find a place to ride?"

"The therapeutic riding center outside the village. They need help exercising their horses, so I volunteered."

Cassie's eyes widened. "Riding One and All?"

By the look of Luke's smile, Cassie knew he'd found a little piece of heaven. "That's the place."

"What a perfect fit for you."

"I know," Luke beamed a wide smile. "Riding helps to clear my head and refocus. Just so you're aware, I have no clue where to buy a gift for Bobby. I'm counting on you."

Cassie liked the sound of that. "Perfect. I have a great idea as long as you're open-minded." Cassie paused. She had to add the disclaimer. She'd promised Conrad. "Listen, there's something I need to make clear."

"Oh?" Luke turned to face her. She took in the details of how smart he looked in the crisp white cotton coat with his name embroidered under the clinic's logo.

"Conrad said this isn't a date." She'd blurted out the words like a schoolgirl in front of her first crush. It must've sounded like one ridiculous long word instead of a sentence. Why had she made such a silly promise to her brother?

Luke snorted a chuckle. He returned her gaze with mischief in his eyes. In a split second, Cassie saw an older version of the man, still attractive with lines etched across his face, still the sweet man underneath. She rubbed her eyes, blaming the vision on her active imagination.

"Right. Friends helping friends kind of thing. I get it." Cassie followed as he resumed his pace down the hall. "Let me get Ruby's med for you, and I'll check you out."

With Luke behind the counter, Cassie grinned. "*You're* checking me out?" Maybe this was another example of one of the changes Luke wanted to make.

Luke threw her a look. "Yeah, I'm a bit of a jack-of-all-trades for a while. Another long story."

Cassie pulled her wallet from her purse and handed

him her credit card. "I know what you mean. I had a long conversation with my accountant the other day. Seems I need to generate a steady income over the off-season or risk going bankrupt."

Before Luke swiped her card, he paused. "We have a payment plan for our customers if that would help."

Cassie waved an OK. "I'm exaggerating the bankruptcy part, you can go ahead and run the card. But I am guilty of dipping into my savings when sales drop over the winter. My accountant's right, I can't keep doing that."

Looking relieved and concerned at the same time, Luke returned the card. "No, probably not."

"I guess I'm not the natural entrepreneur like the rest of my family."

"From what I've seen so far, you'll figure things out."

Cassie slipped her credit card back into her wallet. "Thanks for the vote of confidence. I hope you're right."

Luke reached for the medication from a cabinet and pulled an information sheet from the printer. He slipped both into a bag and sealed it closed with a staple. "Any ideas so far to help you out with the slow season?"

"Maybe. Have you heard about the Rising Star Competition?"

Luke returned the stapler to the drawer and closed it. "Yeah. The competition for all the new businesses in the county."

"If I'm not too late, I'm going to enter."

"Good idea."

Cassie ran her hand down Ruby's head and back.

"Not mine but my accountant's. He said even the exposure could help me. I plan to register on my way home. I just hope I make it before the deadline."

"Worth a shot. In a way, we're in the same boat. I need to modernize this office from the inside out so it's more attractive to buyers. You're looking at the same furniture since Uncle Russ opened the place four decades ago."

Cassie scanned the lobby. "You're right. And those curtains could use an update."

Luke shook his head against the idea. "That's a no. I talked with him about that years ago, but he was resistant to taking them down. Said my aunt made them herself on her sewing machine."

"That's sweet and you know it."

"Yeah." He handed her the med bag for Ruby. "Three pills the first day, then once a day until they're gone. Peanut butter helps. I'd like to see her back for her vaccinations next week."

Cassie smiled. "Thanks so much." She stroked her dog's hair. "Ready to head home, Ruby?"

Although not up for her happy dance, Ruby pulled on the leash in the direction of the door.

"Bye Ruby. See you on Friday for our shopping trip, Cass."

"Sounds good." Cassie turned from the doorway intending to say goodbye until she noticed a yellow ticket on Luke's windshield. *Oh-oh. Should I tell him?*

"Ah, I hate to tell you this, but do you know you have a parking ticket on your Jeep?"

Luke tilted his head upward as if praying for patience. "I forgot to move the jeep. Doesn't surprise me. Seems to be that kind of day so far."

"You mean one full of surprises?"

Luke closed his eyes and moved his head from side to side.

"Welcome home, Luke." Cassie headed toward her car. *Home.* Maybe that's what Luke needed—a little reminder that once upon a time, he called Sister Bay home, and who better to help him? She thought twice about that idea. For now, she had bigger problems to solve. Figuring out how her café would survive over the slow season was at the top of her list. Luke would have to wait.

Chapter 4

On Friday afternoon, Luke headed for the café to pick up Cassie. He never saw this coming— baby gift shopping. She was bundled up in a cream-colored woolen jacket that complimented her warm eyes and dark hair. Ruby trotted right behind her. They were an adorable sight.

"Would you mind company? I hate to leave her all alone." Ruby wore a pink and white knitted jacket, and Luke could've sworn she was proud of it as she pranced alongside her owner.

"Not at all, she's more than welcome. Looks like you're already feeling better." Luke said to the pup.

After settling Ruby in the backseat, Cassie took the seat next to Luke in front. "She is. You always carry a doctor's bag with you?"

Luke smiled. She must've spotted his black bag on top of the car blanket he carried for emergencies. "I do. It's good practice. You never know when an animal may need help."

"Hmm. You sound just like your uncle now."

Luke's shoulders sagged. He hoped this conversation wouldn't lead to the decision to sell the clinic. The topic was becoming a wet blanket. He decided to change the subject. "How did it go at the café today?"

Cassie placed her purse on the floor. "Today was good, but I can feel the slowdown already. Thank goodness the Fall Festival's coming up. I'm hoping for high sales."

"I'm sure you will. I used to love walking from one food vendor to the next, sampling a little from each one. I even enjoyed the activities they planned. It's a great event." Luke turned the radio on to his favorite country station, hoping Cassie would enjoy it.

"Are you talking about the fish boil?" Cassie was well aware of how many visitors clambered to Door County for its popular white fish and garden potato dinner.

Luke wrinkled up his nose. "Not the fish more like the cherry pie."

Cassie chuckled. "Right. Who doesn't? I chose my Door County Chocolate Cherry blend for the day's special."

"Smart. We decided to offer free eye checks at the clinic on the morning of the festival to increase our foot traffic and promote preventative health. As pets get older, they run a risk for cataracts, macular degeneration, and glaucoma."

"Eye checks are a great idea. I plan to keep track of my best sellers so I'm prepared for next year."

Luke exhaled. "I wish we had accountability like that at the clinic. Uncle Russ still uses paper and pencil receipts and a chalkboard for the appointment schedule. There's so much I need to do to bring the practice into the twenty-first century." It wasn't like him to complain, but he had a mountain of work ahead of him to get the clinic up to par.

"I feel your pain. I was so intimidated by all of the incoming and outgoing expenses that I needed to track for my business. Andrea helped me get set up with user-friendly accounting software. I'd be happy to email you the program if you think it could help. It's very user-friendly."

Luke turned the wheel and followed the curve of the highway toward Gills Rock, remembering it was one of the most scenic roads in the state. "That'd be great. Andrea, huh? Chet's fiancé?"

"Mm-hmm. She's a whiz at that stuff. She helped me with marketing ideas too. It's all about cross-marketing for me but even that takes a hit over winter. I'll need something brand-new to help me get through that season."

"I'm looking forward to meeting the woman who captured Chet's heart. She sounds multi-talented."

"I think the world of Andrea. You will too after you meet her."

"I'm sure you're right. Last time we talked, you mentioned entering the Rising Star contest. Did you make it before the deadline to enter?"

"I did." Cassie's hands folded across her chest.

By the sound of it, Luke wasn't sure she was comfortable with the idea. "Are you second-guessing that decision?"

"I'm not sure what the judges will think when they learn that my sales slow over the winter."

From Luke's perspective, Cassie had become a woman of grit and hard-working determination. "Be honest and open. Let them know your situation and that you're willing to do whatever it takes to make your business a success."

He hoped his advice would help her through a difficult truth. His uncle had always stressed honesty before all else, especially in business. She turned and gave him a smile that warmed him. "Wouldn't that be admitting that my business is in trouble?" She unzipped her coat and slipped it from her shoulders. Luke smiled, grateful he thought of clicking on the seat warmers before she got in the vehicle.

"Maybe. But I suspect they'd admire you for disclosing that kind of information." Her gaze moved to the window. It would take a good amount of courage for her to reveal that part of her business, but Luke suspected she was giving his idea some thought.

He glanced in the rearview mirror, turned the corner, and left most of the traffic behind them. "Any thoughts on the perfect gift for Bobby?" Luke was so grateful for Cassie's help. He didn't want to disappoint the little guy.

Her voice lifted. "Bobby is just like his daddy, rough and tough. Most toddlers his age walk around with a security blanket. Not my little nephew. For him, it's a rubber toy hammer. He even sleeps with it."

Luke wished he could capture the wind chime sound of her laughter. He liked it. "That sounds like Conrad's boy."

Luke felt the light touch of her fingers on his arm. He liked that too.

"There's a soft side to him, too. He cuddles into you when you wrap his yellow blanket around him and rock him in Lila's chair."

Cassie's description of Conrad's little guy had him smiling. He visualized Cassie in a cushy chair, soothing the little guy in her arms.

"So, do you think it's a good idea?" Cassie threw him a questioning look.

Oh-oh. How long did I drift off? "Ah…yeah, whatever you think will work." He hoped that was the right answer.

"Did you even hear what I said? You've got an I-don't-know-what-she's-talking about look on your face."

"I think so. Bobby likes soft things?"

"Okay," Cassie said, a hint of suspicion in her voice. "That's close. I was saying that Charlie and Sally McPherson are dear friends of mine. They have an adorable llama farm. Sally has a God-given talent for knitting, crocheting, and sewing. She's already helped me out quite a bit with my quilting projects. Her husband, Charlie, is now a hobby woodworker. He builds most of the toys for the Christmas Giveaway event every year. I thought maybe you could find a workbench or wagon, or something like that, and I'll choose something Sally handmade. And, we'll be supporting local artists. We both know how important that is around here."

Luke had forgotten how the community depended on each other for survival, despite all his uncle had shared with him over the years. "So, Washington Island?" He'd only been there a handful of times. He glanced at his watch. It was a few minutes before three o'clock.

"I can tell by the look on your face that you're concerned we won't make it back in time for the last ferry. Don't be. We'll have plenty of time, and we'll end up with the perfect gifts."

Luke tipped his head toward her. "I'm trusting you on this one. Here we are." Luke pulled onto the Island Clipper ferry at exactly three o'clock still trying to make sense of what had happened to him a moment ago. He'd been super busy since his arrival, especially the last few days trying to reorganize the office. Maybe all he needed was a good night's rest.

~

Cassie knew The Washington Island Ferry typically ran on time. When they disembarked from the ferry and arrived on the island at three-thirty, she directed Luke straight to the McPherson farm. She didn't expect selecting gifts would take long, but she didn't want to make them late by refreshing Luke's memory with sightseeing on the island.

A pea-graveled driveway led them to a two-story white farmhouse with gray shutters. A barn in matching colors was behind the main house. Both buildings were topped with the popular red-tin roofs that dotted the Door County countryside. The same pea-gravel created a loose path from the house to the barn.

Luke whistled, bringing a smile to Cassie's face. "This is nice." He turned off the jeep's engine. "I wouldn't be surprised to see a yoga instructor come out to greet us."

Cassie chuckled. "I thought you might have this reaction. I'm not surprised. Most people in your shoes have the same first impression when I bring them to the McPherson farm." She opened the back door and Ruby sprung from her seat and headed toward the llama pen.

"My shoes? What do you mean?"

Cassie closed the jeep door and started the trek to

the house. She'd spotted Sally at the window when they pulled up and expected she'd be out to greet them any minute. "You know, stressed out." She heard Luke's footsteps right behind her.

"Me? Stressed out?" Luke chuckled. "I don't think so."

Right. "Okay, let's call it heavily preoccupied." Timing it almost perfectly. Cassie left little room for Luke to respond.

"Cassie, it's so good to see you." Cassie's friend, who always reminded her of her favorite celebrity cook gave her a warm embrace. She turned to face Luke and then waited for an introduction.

Cassie turned toward Luke. "Sally, this is Luke Hunter, Russ Hunter's nephew."

Sally's face lit up in a warm smile. She extended a hand and shook Luke's with a bit more enthusiasm than needed. "Good to meet you, Luke. We heard all about you from your uncle when we took our Lulu in for a pre-delivery check-up at the clinic. He's so proud of you."

"Ah," Luke smiled. "He brought me up to speed on Lulu as well."

"Of course he did. You're the new vet who's going to take over the practice, once Russ retires. That poor man struggling with that wicked arthritis. Your arrival is well-timed."

Cassie held her breath as she waited for Luke to correct Sally's assumption.

He didn't. Instead, he threw her a genuine smile. "Thank you, Sally. It's nice to meet you."

Sally folded her arms across her chest. "Cassie's already told me you'd like a gift from Charlie's wood shop. I'm going to send you down to the barn. You'll find him whittling away at a new project down there. You can take a look around and pick out a gift from his collection if you'd like. Just introduce yourself but speak up." Sally pointed to her left ear. "Suffers from hearing loss working on the family egg farm for too many years."

"See you in a bit," Cassie said.

Luke gave her a wink and followed the path to the barn while Cassie joined Sally toward the house. Having changed one of the bedrooms upstairs into a hobby room, Sally led them to what she endearingly called her hobby haven.

Cassie's breath caught when she walked into the room. An array of beautifully hand-knitted items were stacked on shelves arranged as a bookcase spreading across one of the walls. Jumpers, hats, mittens, and more hung from a clothesline strung across the room. Small quilts on a nearby table. Where to start? "Wow. This is going to be tougher than I thought."

Sally smiled. "Hearing that never gets old. Take your time and look around."

Cassie steered her attention to the baby section. She caressed the delicate handiwork of blankets, sleepers, tiny hats, and booties. Fifteen minutes later she felt more torn than when she walked through the door. *Is this how Luke is feeling right about now?*

Hand on her chest, she looked over at Sally already busy behind her sewing machine. "Help," she whimpered. "I'm drowning in all of this loveliness here. You'd better help me make a decision, or I'll never get us out of here on time."

Sally chuckled and opened a lower drawer on her

sewing table. She handed Cassie a garment wrapped in tissue paper. "Take a look at this," she said.

Cassie lifted the paper to reveal a powder-blue pair of knit overhauls with a navy embroidered edge. Between the child-sized fasteners, the name Bobby was centered perfectly in vibrant mandarin-orange stitching. Cassie lifted her eyes to meet those of Sally's. "This is amazing. I've never seen knit overhauls."

Sally folded her arms across her chest with Cassie's reaction. "When you told me that Bobby was just like his daddy, I searched through my pattern books and this one jumped out at me. Don't feel any pressure to take it."

"Are you kidding? It's perfect. It's so original and unique. Thank you, Sally, truly."

A wide smile spread across Sally's face. "I'll wrap it up for you."

After Cassie paid for the item, they made their way back to the main floor and slipped on their jackets.

"Sooo, what's going on between you and the handsome doctor?"

"Not much," Cassie quickly replied. "We grew up together and now we're friends."

"Ah-ha," Sally chuckled.

Cassie knew she didn't believe that for a second.

Sally waggled a finger. "You two have that thingy going on. I saw it from the window already."

Cassie glared at her longtime friend. "Thingy? You lost me."

Sally playfully bumped Cassie's shoulder with her own. "They used to call it electricity. A magnetic force between two people when the stars align."

Cassie moaned. "Oh, my, this does sound serious."

"Hard to deny if I picked up on it that quickly. From both of you, I might add."

Cassie looked at her with irritation. "Not interested. One heartbreak in a lifetime is enough for me."

"You always said you wouldn't give love a second chance, but you might reconsider in this case. You just haven't met him yet, until now, maybe."

"Ugh," Cassie uttered. *Not with a guy who's not sticking around.* Electricity or not, no one would stop that freight train of dreams from moving forward.

Sally's light touch rubbed Cassie's back. "Don't be so quick to throw in the towel."

Cassie opened her mouth to defend her point of view, but Sally being Sally, had beaten her to it. "Now let's go see what our men are up to."

Chapter 5

A half-hour later, Luke and Cassie were headed back to the ferry dock. With Ruby sound asleep in the backseat after an afternoon of chasing llamas, Cassie suggested she and Luke enjoy the trip back to the mainland on the boat's second-floor viewing deck. They sat side-by-side on a wooden bench with a handful of other passengers, hoping to catch Wisconsin's final push of autumn color.

With sunset upon them, a mist-like fog lifted from the water, causing Cassie to shiver.

"Maybe this will help." Luke unfolded the woolen car blanket he'd brought along from the Jeep. Cassie leaned forward, providing him the room to drape it around her shoulders.

"Thank you." Cassie peered into the water landscape ahead thankful for the blanket's warmth. "I like to take time to say goodbye to summer every year. The ferry ride back gives me the perfect opportunity."

Luke turned up the collar on his coat, and Cassie noted neither one of them wore a hat or gloves. "Not a fan of the cold weather?"

She snuggled under the blanket thankful for Luke's thoughtfulness. "I wouldn't say that. I love leaving my bedroom window open a crack and cuddling under a thick quilt at night. It's one of my favorite seasons, right after spring, summer, and winter."

"So, basically, you love them all." Luke chuckled.

"I guess so. Each year the seasons introduce another part of God's world that I hadn't noticed the year before."

"I love the outdoors and never miss an opportunity to go horseback riding, but I never thought about saying goodbye to a season. I guess when you're raised by gypsies there's little time for nostalgia."

Cassie chuckled, enjoying Luke's strong sense of humor. "Your parents are hardly gypsies."

"Nomads then?" Luke arched a brow with his question.

Cassie picked up on the hint of mischief in his voice. "It sounds like your parents moved a lot, but home is where they are."

"Home," Luke repeated, wearing a faraway look on his face. He tipped his head to the sky as if to examine the early onset of twilight's cloud cover. "The closest I came to having any semblance of a normal life was when I started coming up here every summer. If it wouldn't have been for Uncle Russ, that wouldn't have happened."

"What do you mean?"

Luke shrugged. "My parents didn't see the value in it. I don't know how he managed to convince them, but I'm glad he did. There was a predictability to the way Uncle Russ ran his life—vaccinations on the first Saturday of every month, wellness checks on Thursdays, and his haircut every fourth Friday at noon. That sort of thing. In a way, it grounded me for the first time in my life. I was bored at times, but content too."

"Yet, by going after the PetsAmerica job you've decided to follow your parent's lifestyle."

She heard his huff and saw the question in his eyes. "What?"

Cassie's shoulders caved. Once again, she'd overstepped. She'd better be quick with an explanation. "Isn't that what you're doing by seeking a job that offers relocation every three years." It didn't make any sense to Cassie. At times, Luke sounded as if he wanted the exact opposite.

"I see. Conrad must've filled you in on the details of the job with PetsAmerica, huh?"

Cassie lifted her chin to cool down her embarrassed cheeks. *When will I learn to be more subtle?* "He did, yes. I hope you don't mind."

Luke gave a shoulder shrug. "Nah. For as long as I can remember, it's been ingrained in me to keep reaching for the stars and not settle for the status quo. With a new employment contract every three years, the job with PetsAmerica will help me do that."

"Hmpf." Cassie didn't get it. "Is that your new motto for life? No disrespect to your parents, but that almost sounds a bit ungrateful." She winced at the words that fell from her lips and prepared for his rebuttal.

Instead, Luke went quiet. For a moment she thought she'd gone too far until she heard a long-winded whistle. *That's the second time today. Now, he's a whistler?* Maybe he'd picked that up, like the cowboy hat and boots, from the years living in Nashville.

"Man, you really let a guy have it, don't you?" He

leaned forward resting his arms on his thighs.

Oh no. Cassie turned her scalded face to the wind, grateful now for its icy chill. No wonder she needed her brother's help to find her dates. Not that she accepted any of his suggestions. She pulled the blanket up to her nose, doing her best to hide her embarrassment. "I'm sorry. You remember how free I am with my opinions. I apologize if I've overstepped. Seems to be a grooved-in habit of mine."

She felt his weight shift—the warmth of his body so close to hers. Not sure what to expect, she peeked over her shoulder at him, meeting his steel gray blues head-on, and found him smiling. *Smiling!*

"I like it. Always have. Keeps a guy accountable."

Is he serious? Her last breakup, the one that tore her heart into shreds, had taught her he probably wasn't. "History has proven otherwise."

"Hmm. Then he wasn't the right guy for you."

Not wanting to open up the topic, Cassie chose another. "What's first on your to-do list for the clinic?" This ought to move the conversation in another direction.

Luke scoffed. "I discovered one of the examining rooms has water damage in the ceiling and walls. I need a drywaller first and then I'll need to paint. I'd like to get new laminate in all of the rooms, including the waiting area. Hopefully, there's money left over for some new furniture. The plastic chairs in the waiting area have to go."

"Wow. I thought I had my hands full getting the café ready for the contest coming up. You're going to be busy."

"Speaking of that, when does the contest begin? I

would imagine it'll take some time for the committee to make their decision."

"The judges are making their stops next week already. Winners will be announced at the Fall Festival after the Pink Pumpkin Race."

"I'll be rooting for you. I'm glad you brought up the race. Any chance you're looking for a partner?"

Cassie drew a blank. "I wasn't planning on participating." *Is he asking me out?* Even though she found him attractive and easy to be with, she'd sworn off dating after her heart was stepped on more than a year ago.

"Oh, come on. I'm not half-bad in a gunny-sack," he laughed.

Cassie grinned. He *is* asking me out. "Okay." What harm could come from a gunny-sack race? That's not really a date.

The ferry pivoted in preparation for docking, hitting an oncoming wave. An ice-cold spray headed in their direction. Instinctively, Cassie turned to Luke, sliding behind his shoulder, and slipping her arm under his. She felt the pressure of his arm over hers. He snuggled her in nice and tight. Eyes closed, Cassie buried her face in Luke's shoulder, turning away from the oncoming water blitz headed straight for them. Luke bent his head to cover hers. "Ah!" they both screamed.

"I just happen to bring them along," Luke said, pulling a pair of gloves from his pocket. Placing his arms around her, he dabbed at the water droplets from her hair and coat.

By instinct, she brushed a fingertip across the scar over his eyebrow. "You'd better be careful or you'll end up getting clobbered again like you did with that wayward swing."

"Better me than you, both then and now."

His words left her speechless, a rare occurrence. Instead, Sally's comment echoed in her head.

No. No. No. We do not have a thingy going on. He's moving on. Leaving Sister Bay as soon as the clinic sells, and I'm not shopping around for another heartbreak. The absolute worst idea would be to fall for a guy who doesn't plan to stay.

Chapter 6

The following evening, Luke stood outside Conrad and Lila's home awestruck by the diameter of the log-built structure. He could only imagine the determination and long hours Conrad must have endured in constructing such a large, beautiful house. The company he had dreamed about as a kid had come into reality for him. The two-story cabin, if you could call it that, was magnificent and stood on a wooded pine lot as if it had been there as long as the age-old trees.

Leaves swirled around Luke's feet. Their music reminded him to keep moving. *What's your problem, Hunter?* He drew in a heavy breath. There was a time when he easily fit in with this community of people. But now, with his decision to sell the clinic on everyone's mind, he wasn't sure.

The warm, twinkling lights inside lured Luke closer. He pressed the birthday gift for Bobby against his chest, climbed the short stack of stairs, and rang the bell.

The door swooshed open, and Lila gave him a radiant smile that extinguished Luke's hesitation on the spot. Her Aunt Cathy stood right behind her.

Remembering Lila had lost both parents years ago in a fatal car accident, it didn't surprise him to find her aunt close by her side.

"Luke, I can't tell you how good it is to see you," Lila said in a warm voice. "Come in out of the cold."

Luke gave Lila the best hug he could while maintaining his hold on the gift.

After Aunt Cathy secured a bunch of balloons marked "Happy Birthday" to a nearby table, she stepped toward him. "Here, let me help you with that, Luke. I'll place it on the gift table for you and be right back."

"Thank you, Cathy," Luke said, then he turned toward Lila. "I hope Bobby likes it. It's a Noah's Ark train set. I picked it out from Charlie McPherson's woodshop. Each train car has a pair of animals in it."

Lila closed the door behind him."You went all the way to Washington Island for Bobby's gift?" The lift in her voice told Luke he'd impressed her.

"I can't take all the credit. Cassie suggested we make the trip. It was all her idea."

Lila shook her head. "She's always thinking outside of the box. Can you believe the talent Sally and Charlie have under one roof? Or should I say, two, counting Charlie's woodshop?"

Aunt Cathy returned and bobbed her head in agreement, having heard Lila's question. "I ordered a few Christmas gifts for Bobby from Sally's hobby haven. The detail in her work makes a one-of-a-kind gift."

Luke agreed, having been impressed with the outfit Cassie had purchased for the little guy. "Ruby enjoyed herself too, chasing the llamas around," Luke added.

The two women laughed, relaxing the tightness in Luke's shoulders. He was already enjoying himself. "Even the trip back to the mainland was nice, despite the dip in temperature. The color in the trees was outstanding."

Cathy agreed with an, "Ah," as if there were more to share. A memory sprang to mind of how she and Conrad's mother teamed up to help Lila and Conrad's relationship along. Luke swallowed hard. As a single, eligible bachelor, Luke hoped he wasn't next on their matchmaking list.

"Did your uncle come with you?" Lila asked. "I was hoping he could take a peek at Chester."

Cathy stepped forward, closing in on the conversation. Her eyes were glued to him.

"No, I'm sorry he wasn't feeling up to it tonight. He sends his regrets."

Luke picked up on disappointment from Cathy from the look on her face. "What's going on with Chester?" he asked Lila.

A set of lines deepened Lila's forehead.

Luke hoped it wasn't anything serious with their rescue. "I'd be happy to take a look."

"He's developed a bit of a limp over the past few days." Lila's look turned serious.

"Okay, I always carry my doctor's bag in the car. Let me…"

Lila placed a hand on Luke's shoulder, stopping his next step toward the door. "It's not the first time this has happened. Why don't you enjoy the party, and before you leave, you can take a peek? I'm sure you're anxious to reconnect with everyone here."

Luke paused. "If you insist."

"I do, Dr. Hunter," Lila said with a wink. She gestured for his coat and left him to mingle.

The aroma of barbequed beef drifted through the room, luring Luke to an enormous banquet table decked out with salads, savory meat, and casseroles. He spotted a three-layered birthday cake decked out with white and blue icing with a plastic toy tractor on top. *What a spread!* He was about to fill a plate but couldn't avoid a shoulder-to-shoulder collision with one of the other guests.

"How long was it going to take you to say hello?"

Luke recognized the gruff voice in an instant and found his friend, Chet Taylor, standing in his path. *His strong sense of humor is still in full swing.* Luke shot his shoulders back and stood tall. "What are you talking about? I just got here." He stuck out his hand and grabbed his friend's in a strong handshake.

Chet looked good. Strong as usual from the laborious tasks on his family farm and B&B. A petite, stunning woman with jet-black hair stood beside him. "I heard you were back in town. I want you to meet my fiancé. Luke Hunter this is Andrea Lockhart, my one and only."

Andrea's blue-violet eyes twinkled at Chet and then at Luke. After a quick handshake, Andrea slipped her hand back into Chet's. His fingers wrapped around hers.

"I've heard a lot about you, Luke. It's nice to finally meet you."

"It's a pleasure, Andrea. I'm looking forward to your wedding."

"Did you hear about the dance competition?" Chet emptied the contents of his glass.

Luke lifted a brow. "Yup. A little unconventional, isn't it?"

Chet shot him a half-smile. "Did you expect anything different?"

Luke chuckled. " From you, my friend. Ah, no."

"We wanted to jazz up the evening and have everyone celebrating with us right up until the end." Andrea leaned against Chet.

"You got a date? Otherwise, maybe Andrea can hook you up with one of her New York friends." Chet gave him an inquiring look.

Andrea giggled as if the suggestion of Luke needing a date was ridiculous. He liked her for that.

"Yeah, I got a date. Cassie."

Chet's eyebrows rose. "Hamilton?" he barked, causing a few heads to turn in their direction.

Luke shrugged a shoulder to ease the looks of concern. *He hasn't changed.* Boisterous, proud, and a bit arrogant with his opinions were all dead-on markers that made Chet Taylor who he was.

But Chet was dead wrong now on what his tone had implied. Luke raised a hand to stop any further assumptions. "Listen, it's not really a date. She calls it a "plus-one". Whatever that is." Luke glanced around the room. *Where's Cassie?*

Andrea's question pulled him back to the conversation. "She actually said a plus-one?"

Luke wasn't sure where Cassie was at this point, and he certainly didn't want her to know he was still clueless about the term. He leaned toward Andrea and lowered his voice. "What's your take on the definition of a plus-one? Cassie said it's like going as friends. Does that mean I meet her there or pick her up?"

Andrea smiled. "That's to be decided between you. Plus-one is a no-pressure situation."

Chet snorted. "Oh, come on, Babe. Don't give him some fancy-schmancy writer's definition. Luke's a nuts-and-bolts kind of guy, like me." He shot Luke an us-guys-need-to-stick together look that Luke quickly acknowledged. The old feeling of knowing and being known wrapped around him, extinguishing the fires of his earlier concerns and welcoming him back into the fold of his friends' lives.

Andrea stepped forward toward Luke. "It means there are no expectations for either one of you. You're there for each other instead of going alone. I always liked the idea."

Chet cocked his head in Andrea's direction. "You won't be enjoying that thought for long after I slip that ring on your finger." He chuckled afterward, clearly enjoying his sense of humor.

Andrea patted Chet's arm. "Oh, Chet. I'm not referring to myself here."

His friend's arm slid around Andrea's shoulders, pulling her close. He pushed aside a long sparkly earring with a finger and whispered something in her ear that blushed her cheeks cherry-red.

An unfamiliar desire crept into Luke's heart when he realized they'd captured the magic.

"Luke, over here," Conrad's voice traveled across the room from the kitchen.

Luke threw Conrad a nod and told Chet and Andrea, he'd see them later. As he made his way across the grand gathering space, many of the faces looked familiar, some were new. Many were couples. His mind wandered back to Cassie. Would she come alone tonight? He didn't imagine she would. What guy wouldn't want to be at her side? She had it all going on, both personally and professionally.

As he made his way to the kitchen, he stopped to shake hands with old acquaintances, listen to a joke, or jot down a reminder on a notepad about a pet concern. With his uncle's absence, it felt as if he were slipping into the older man's shoes. It unexpectedly welcomed Luke back into the community.

As soon as he turned the corner and entered the kitchen, Conrad grasped his hand in a firm handshake. "Hey, man, glad you made it. This is probably the last place a single dude like you wants to be."

"Are you kidding me? I wouldn't have missed it. Where's this little man of yours?" He couldn't wait to meet the son Conrad couldn't stop gushing about.

Conrad motioned to the other side of the kitchen. "Right over there, in the arms of his godmother."

Luke tracked Conrad's gaze to a shadowy niche where a woman sat in a cushioned rocking chair, head bent low toward the baby in her arms. A soft light cast a warm glow on the pair. Luke squinted, adjusting his eyes to the dimly lit figures. Her foot stopped the slow easy cadence of the chair.

Cassie peered up at him with a soft smile, and Luke's world rocked way off-kilter.

Conrad's strong hand patted Luke forward. "Well, don't be shy. Lila just fed him, so he's a happy camper now."

Luke shot Conrad a weak smile. If only he could get rid of the cement from his feet, securing him to the floor. *Move, man.* What was his problem?

Watching Cassie holding this curly-haired one-year-old hit him all wrong. He wasn't sure what to do with this surge of…what? Emotions? He looked around the room for something cold to drink. He had to reset his internal barometer and clear his head.

Bobby was snuggled against Cassie so close and so tight that Luke could see the love that radiated from her to him. The baby's pudgy hand was wrapped around one of her fingers.

Something warm roared through Luke, filling the cracks and crevices that made him who he was. It moved in the direction of that snowcapped mountain he'd always envisioned as his philosophy, doing life alone.

It is the best plan. This is how he'd be able to travel every three years. It was the reason why he was pursuing the job with PetsAmerica. Despite the confusing thoughts flying through his head, Luke stepped toward Cassie and the baby. He wanted a closer look.

"Is he already wearing your gift?"

Cassie grinned. "I couldn't wait." Excitement danced across her face. She gave him a look that grounded him, reminding him of living life with his uncle. She lifted Bobby in his direction.

Luke wasn't ready for the impact of Bobby's luminous blue eyes. "Wh-where did he get those big blue eyes?" Both Conrad and Lila had deep brown hues.

Cassie grinned. "Lila said from her dad. It's so fitting that Bobby carries his namesake, isn't it? They had no idea he'd have her father's eyes when they chose his name."

"Yeah, what a coincidence." Luke wished he knew

more about genetics and inherited traits.

"I don't believe in coincidences."

Her comment didn't surprise him. "And you're his godmother?"

Cassie beamed, clearly all in with the lifelong commitment to her nephew.

"Conrad had planned on asking you to be Bobby's godfather."

"Me?" Luke felt the blood drain from his face. If only he could offer more than a weak response. His life had turned upside down since he arrived back in the village. The clinic should've been sold by now, and he'd be on his way to the final interview and to begin a brand-new career. Why this unexpected twist?

"When he found out you didn't plan to stick around, he asked Chet."

Luke fought an unexpected surge of regret. With the future he had in his sights, friendships, as he had here, would be far and few between.

Cassie placed Bobby in his arms. The baby immediately bopped Luke's nose with his toy rubber hammer, glossed over with baby drool.

Luke shifted his head to avoid a second blow while Cassie reached for a soft cloth.

Cassie moved closer. "He doesn't realize what he's doing."

Luke chuckled "I know. I just didn't see it coming."

Their eyes danced together, and Luke marveled at the pretty specks of gold in Cassie's irises again. Her soft brown hair lay in long curls down her shoulders and back.

Luke rounded his chest. He hoped she couldn't

hear the thudding of his heart.

"I always have this close at hand." She dabbed the wet spots from Luke's nose and cheeks using a light touch.

His lips curled at her quick thinking. He looked down at his best friend's son awestruck by the miracle of birth. What a joy it must be to conceive a child with the woman you love. *An absolute miracle.*

Chet strode into the room. "It looks good on you." He grabbed two cups of hot cider from the kitchen counter.

Luke raised a brow. "Huh?" He looked over his shoulder at his friend. "What're you talking about?"

"Daddyhood," Chet teased. "I may have beat you to the altar, but you may be miles ahead of me on this one."

Luke shot Chet a you've-got-to-be-kidding look.

"Life has a mind of its own you know," Chet said. "And I'm picking a front-row seat to yours."

"Get outta' here," Luke jeered and turned his attention back to Bobby who seemed fascinated by a button on his shirt.

Cassie threw Chet a scolding look, then turned back to face Luke. "Are you enjoying the party?"

"I am. It's nice to be back. I spent the last hour talking to several people about their pet situations. I think Uncle Russ has been letting things slide for too long."

"I'm sure they know their pets will be well taken care of now that you're back."

"You bet they will. It's not going to help me sell the clinic if the customers are unhappy. I've got my work cut out for me."

He saw the change in Cassie's face but was unable to read it.

"I'm glad to hear it. Did Lila tell you about Chester?"

"She did. I think I'll take a quick peek now that the party's winding down a bit."

"I'll show you where he is." Cassie lifted Bobby from his arms.

Luke's felt the emptiness with the absence of the child. What was wrong with him tonight?

"I think the festivities have worn this little guy out." She placed the sleepy boy in his pack-and-play and drew a blue elephant blanket snugly around him.

As he watched Bobby slide his thumb into his mouth, eyelids now heavy, another piece of Luke's snowy mountain avalanched into the water.

The sooner the clinic sold, the better.

Chapter 7

Cassie had trouble staying focused, even though it was a little after eight o'clock on a typical Friday morning. The café was full, but not as robust compared to the summer season. Maybe the distraction was Luke, who sat at the counter. Since the party at Conrad's, he'd habitually stopped in every morning. He told Cassie his reason was that his Uncle Russ loved her coffee specials and a muffin or scone for breakfast.

Luke pushed his cup toward her. "So, what about the dance lessons?"

From behind the counter, Cassie poured him a second cup of coffee. She placed his favorite pecan scone in front of him. "It was *Chet* who told you about the dance studio?" She had trouble believing this was true.

"Yup. He told me the studio is just outside the village. I think we'd better sign up." Luke slid the plate closer and eyed the pastry.

Cassie threw him a blank look. "As hard as I try, I can't see Chet Taylor in a dance class."

"Chet and Andrea have a private lesson. It's separate from the group we'd be in. We'd better count on taking at least two, maybe three classes a week to catch up with the others."

"Mm-hmm." Cassie didn't intend to sound disinterested but the judges for the Rising Star Contest could walk through her door at any moment. She and Zoey had worked until midnight. They scrubbed the sink until it shone, polished the floors, and reorganized the pantry. The café should pass with flying colors, yet despite it all, it offered little consolation for her concern about the down season. *How will I handle that question if I'm asked?*

As if she willed it to happen, the bell tinkled overhead, alerting her that new customers had arrived. There in the doorway stood two women with clipboards in their hands. *They're here.*

"Remember to breathe," Luke said loud enough for her to hear but no one else.

Was he warning her to think before she spoke today, a habit she had yet to master? Cassie took a few steps toward the kitchen and peeked her head inside. "Zoey, you're in charge for a while."

"I'm on it." Zoey's voice carried loud and clear.

Cassie took Luke's advice and drew in a breath. *I'm ready. With a fresh* smile, she headed in the judges' direction.

"Good morning, ladies." Cassie read the name badges clipped to the lapels of their coats—*Mrs. Dorothy Ellis, Judge, Mrs. Rita Hall, Judge.* "Please, let me take your coats."

"You must be Cassie, the owner?" Mrs. Ellis asked.

"That's right. I'm Cassie Hamilton. I'd like to welcome you both to The Perfect Cup." The pleasant tone in her voice would be hard to miss. The judges darkened the first circle on their evaluation forms. Cassie hoped it was the right one.

Cassie led the way through the cozy café, each table dressed in pretty, linen tablecloths and complimentary flowers. She explained how the small dining room could comfortably seat up to thirty customers. The counter accommodated another eight. For a split second, Cassie froze. She had to highlight what made her café unique, not just what they could see. She couldn't have planned it better as Luke dropped a few quarters into the jukebox. A familiar country ballad played softly in the background, easing her shoulders. *Thank you, Luke.* After a quick smile in Luke's direction, she led the ladies toward the music machine.

"This is quite an unusual addition for a café," Mrs. Hall remarked.

Because the judge's expression was hard to read, Cassie hesitated. Luke's advice reminded her to breathe. "The previous owner preferred not to move it. I wasn't planning on keeping it until I noticed the customers enjoying their favorite songs for the price of a quarter. I was as surprised then as you are now."

Cassie scanned the diner to find everything running smoothly under Zoey's charge. New arriving customers were seated promptly, and Luke tapped his foot to the music as he finished his scone. When he noticed her, he gave her a thumbs-up and an encouraging smile.

As the three women strolled through the dining area, Cassie pointed out the pretty checkerboard curtains and the lanterns that hung from the ceiling. She explained her decision to purchase an electric fireplace at the local thrift shop and how her customers made a beeline for the tables when the temperatures dropped. With the dining room tour complete, Cassie steered them toward the kitchen.

Before she had the chance to share the most important aspects of operating a coffee house, thoughts of Ruby flashed through her mind. *Had Zoey remembered to put her back in the crate? Why hadn't she done that herself when the ladies arrived?* As soon as they turned the corner and walked into the kitchen, her question was answered.

Ruby's head lifted from her tufted pillow bed. Her eyes were wide with excitement. If there was one thing in this world her golden mix loved, it was people, and why she made such a nice addition to the café. In the next blink, her paws were on the ground, and she was heading in their direction. The jingle bells Cassie had added to her collar rang out their tune.

Oh no.

"Oh, my goodness, who do we have here?" Mrs. Ellis lowered herself to the ground to greet the dog, heading straight for her while Mrs. Hall backed away.

Cassie extended her hands to slow Ruby's zeal. "Ruby, sit."

The dog obeyed and plopped on her behind.

Thank you. "Good girl, Ruby. This is Ruby, my one-year-old golden mix. She's my latest addition to the café."

Mrs. Ellis beamed. "What an absolute delight. How do your customers respond to her?" It was obvious she was enjoying the unexpected visit. Ruby remained in a seated position as the judge patted her head.

Mrs. Hall tucked the clipboard under her arm. Her hands clasped together. "I don't care for animals. I was bitten as a child."

Cassie's concern grew. If Mrs. Hall was afraid of dogs, this interview could turn disastrous. She remembered Luke's advice and stalled the first words coming to mind. Instead, she softened her heart. Should she explain the recent movement of leniency to allow dogs in restaurants and stores? *No.* Instead, she decided to add a little humor. "Ruby's a great marketing magnet. There are times I suspect the only reason tourists come into the café is to see her."

When both ladies smiled, Cassie's concern eased. "This past summer, I offered a promotional package, the daily special with a picture of Ruby. It was quite popular. Most of the regulars love her as much as I do. When they come in, they'll ask me if she's working today."

Mrs. Ellis shook her head. "I can just imagine. We have two Yorkies at home. Our grandkids love them." She placed a hand on the island and eased herself back to a standing position.

With the lure of a biscuit, Cassie led Ruby back into her crate and latched the door. She'd been training her new dog with treats and positive reinforcement for good behavior. She wanted Ruby to be part of her life at the café along with a special experience for her customers. But she had to behave. Over the last few weeks, she'd shown significant progress, sitting on command, rolling over, and now learning a few more cue words that would allow her to be in the dining area.

Cassie wished Luke would drop another quarter into the jukebox. Music always had a calming effect on her. "Let's take a look at the coffee machines." She described her daily routine, the roasts she always offered and her special blends, the muffins, and scones she added to the menu, and the hot sandwiches she was considering. The three women now stood behind the counter sampling the day's coffee special. Cassie beamed as their gaze moved to the sparkling clean windows onto Bay Street, the retail hub district of the village.

"One last question," Mrs. Hall placed her cup on the counter and removed the pencil from the clipboard. "How does the winter season affect sales?"

This is it. The question she most dreaded. Her eyes searched the room and rested on Luke. He mouthed the words, "Be honest."

Cassie turned back to the judges. "In all honesty, it's tough, but I keep our winter visitors in mind and their desire for a hot cup of coffee or cocoa after a fun day outdoors. So far, I have fostered co-marketing relationships with other retailers who stay open over the winter months. My coffee blends come from Ernie's Grinds, a local vendor in Sturgeon Bay, who offered to advertise for me. The lavender that you see throughout the diner comes from the farm on Washington Island. In turn, he serves my coffee to the island tourists. The baked goods are from Susie's Sweet Spot on Elm Street. The coffee she serves her customers is from The Perfect Cup. We do as much as we can for each other, but there are times when we need a little help in return, which is one of the reasons I entered the contest. Not only because I love my little café on Bay Street, and I want the whole world to know about it, but I need new opportunities to help it survive the leaner months of the year and become a success down the road."

As Cassie spoke, the pencils in the judge's fingers flew across their papers. Cassie prayed that Luke had been right in his advice.

Mrs. Hall rested a light hand on Cassie's arm. "Young lady, we want to thank you for the wonderful tour of your café and your honesty. Will you be attending the festival when the winners of this competition will be announced? You have to be present to win."

"I wouldn't miss it, ladies. I'll be heading straight over from the Pink Pumpkin race." Cassie handed each of them their coats, along with a blueberry scone tucked into a Perfect Cup to-go bag.

After a quick look at the poster board displaying Ruby with her customers, everyone said their goodbyes. Cassie appreciated Zoey's idea to move the snapshot collage near the entrance as she watched the judges scan the board. A collection of photos that showcased patrons with their cups of coffee and Ruby at their side or their arms around her neck filled the framed poster board.

Mrs. Ellis pointed at the display. "I'll be back for my picture."

Mrs. Hall slipped a pair of brown leather gloves on her hands. "We're not quite finished yet. Remember, we have to stop at the new coffee spot in Gills Rock."

The surprise that there was another contestant hit Cassie like an unsavory brew. As if the incident with Ruby wasn't enough of an unexpected whoops. "There's another contestant in the café category?"

Cassie had made a point to visit the other small diners that entered the competition. She must have missed the one in Gills Rock.

Mrs. Hall draped a patterned scarf over her coat. "They made it right before the deadline. A little coffee drive-thru. It's a brand-new concept for Door County. It's called, oh, wait a minute." She flipped through the pages on her clipboard. "Dock and Go Coffee."

Cassie pressed her lips together. They were probably marketing to the travelers on the ferry. *Good idea.* Why hadn't she noticed it on the trip to Washington Island last week? She held back the negative thoughts that wanted to spoil the judges' visit. "Enjoy the rest of your day, ladies, and come visit again soon."

As soon as the door closed behind them, Luke started clapping, others soon followed his lead.

Sweet man. With two strikes against her, Cassie's view on how the café would do against the other contestants began to fade.

Chapter 8

The following Saturday morning, the Harvest Moon Festival was well underway. Inside the café, the aroma of a dark roast coffee brewed. Cassie stole a quick look outside to find the street filled with festival attendees. Earlier, the village streets had been blocked off, allowing easy access to the artisan booths and shops. Inside the café, it had been standing room only for the last two hours. Cassie and Zoey had been busy bussing trays filled with coffee and pastries.

Cassie remembered the heavily attended morning of the event and decided to take advantage of the foot traffic and the sales. Today she offered two specials, a spiced chai and ham and cheese croissants. She threw in the option to have a snapshot with Ruby for anyone interested. That was the reason she and Zoey were hustling, doing their best to keep up with traffic.

In the kitchen, Cassie filled an empty carafe with Butternut rum coffee, secured the top, and placed it onto her tray. She reached for a small plate of cherry muffins. "Zoey, I've been meaning to tell you what a good idea it was to make up these muffin and scone platters. It's so easy to grab and go. How are the croissant sandwiches holding up?"

"They're a big hit. We're down to a half-dozen. You were dead-on right to add them to today's menu."

Cassie giggled at Zoey's zany sense of humor. *Dead-on right, huh?* "You're a natural in the café business."

Zoey blew a strand of her purple-tinted hair from her eyes. "Must've come from the years working for my aunt's restaurant. I always thought I'd take over when she retired, but she's still loving every minute of it."

Cassie reflected on when the young woman had answered the ad last month. At the time, she questioned if she was ready to hire the unconventional-looking waitress. Dressed in ink-black leggings and a tie-dyed top, Zoey's tinted hair alone would attract attention to her quiet café on Bay Street. But the young woman's previous restaurant experience and warm smile had convinced Cassie to give her a try. Maybe the café needed a boost in the unconventional. So far, the risk Cassie had taken had proven to be the right move. The regular customers enjoyed her unabashed sense of humor, and Cassie was able to serve almost twice as many customers with her help. That would make her accountant smile.

Zoey plated the last of the muffins and then reached for the plastic bin of chocolate chip scones. "What's your gut feeling on the Rising Star Competition?"

"I'm determined to keep a positive attitude and find at least one good outcome from the competition, win or lose."

Zoey slid the bin back into place. "That's the spirit."

Cassie didn't share that she had to remind herself of that positive outlook every day. Deep down, she wasn't so sure how the café would measure up after discovering one of the judges was afraid of Ruby and then finding out about the new coffee drive-through in Gills Rock. She had her doubts. She hoped her accountant was right when he said even the exposure could boost sales.

"I'm off," Cassie called out, and easily lifted the full tray and headed out of the kitchen.

Luke caught her eye. He stood in the doorway doing his best to excuse himself through the line of waiting patrons. He looked as if he just dismounted off a horse. He must've gone riding again. He shot Cassie a defeated look. "See you at the race," he mouthed.

She wanted to give him a thumbs up but all she could manage was a nod and smile. The business was booming this morning, and she couldn't be happier.

~

Once business had slowed a couple of hours later, Cassie locked up after one of the best days she'd had since the grand opening. A warm surge of satisfaction filled her. All the extra work had been worth it. As far as the Rising Star Competition went, she now believed it would end as it was meant to. Right now, she was on top of the world and couldn't wait to tell Luke all about it.

Cassie headed across the street toward the Pink Pumpkin race and had a hard time believing she'd agreed to compete in a gunny sack race. She was definitely in a celebratory mood but to slip into a gunny sack and race? What had she been thinking? Not the most coordinated in her family, this could be comical.

A pink pumpkin flag flapped in the wind, she followed the path toward it and looked out into the sea of racers. Some were in lines waiting for a sack while others were securing their legs with a mini-bungee cord.

"Hey, Cassie, you looking for someone?"

Cassie followed the voice to Chet. He stood with one leg in a gunny sack while steadying an unbalanced Andrea.

"You'd think all those years in ballet would help me out here," Andrea giggled. "Not."

"Just hang on to the big handsome fiancé of yours," Cassie suggested. She grinned at Chet. "What makes you think I'm searching for someone?" she asked him.

"It's obvious by the look on your face."

Conrad pushed through the crowd. Lila, right behind him with Bobby resting on one hip. "What look?" he asked.

Cassie rolled her eyes. Would she ever be free of her overseeing brother and his friends?

Lila smiled in her direction as if she'd read Cassie's mind.

"If you're looking for a partner, I'm available," Conrad offered. He gave a head nod in his wife's direction. "Lila's out this year."

Cassie moaned. She loved her brother dearly but that was the last thing she wanted. Kind-hearted Conrad teams up with his single sister. The whistle blew, signaling all contestants to gather behind the red banner that whipped in the October wind.

Cassie shivered and then zipped up her quilted jacket. If Luke were here, she didn't see him. Until she did. As the contestants moved into their starting positions, he stood alone, scanning the crowd.

Cassie's heart warmed. *He's searching for me.* "Luke!" she shouted over the second announcement.

Jogging in her direction, Luke flashed her a wide smile. "Let's go, partner."

"You again?" remarked Conrad. He wore a perturbed look on his face.

Luke raised his chin. "Yeah, that's right. I talked Cassie into being my partner. After all, we're both solos here."

"Humph." Cassie's overprotective brother threw Luke a questioning glance. "Yeah, okay, but I hope you don't think you're going to win, not if you still have those two left feet of yours."

Chet chuckled. "It can get ugly. We've all seen you dance."

"Oh, stop, you two," Cassie scolded. "This is about working together, which I happen to know is a problem for both of you."

Conrad and Chet must've gotten the hint because they zipped their lips while Luke stepped forward, gunny-sack in hand. "I'll take my chances, two left feet and all."

"Me, too," Cassie slipped her arm into his. "Let's get in line."

Once the bell rang and the racers were off, Cassie forgot all about the comments from Conrad and Chet. With one of their legs bound together, they used their wits to swerve around the other contestants and even managed a jump over a pair who had fallen right in their path. If it hadn't been for Luke, breaking her fall, they would've landed right on top of them. They laughed so hard that Cassie's stomach ached. But it was worth it. They ended up with a second-place win and a red ribbon to prove it.

Chet and Andrea hustled up behind them. "This was Andrea's first time. Wait until next year!"

"Sure, Chet. Blame it on the new girl," Luke jeered.

"That is pretty low, dude," Conrad chuckled, bringing the group to a burst of roaring laughter, including Bobby.

A few minutes later, Cassie said her goodbyes and headed toward the Chamber of Commerce building. The announcement for the Rising Star Competition was the closing event for the day. She didn't want to miss it, whether she won or not. The judges had reminded her that she had to be present to accept a prize. And that positive attitude she'd been holding onto all week had kept her spirits high.

Luke caught up with her. "Hey, I'd like to come along with you, if you don't mind. For moral support if nothing else."

An autumn wind swirled, depositing leaves in their path. Cassie wrapped a knit scarf around her neck and tucked it into her jacket. "That would be nice. I'll admit, I'm a little nervous."

His arm slid around her shoulders and squeezed her.

It felt…nice. Warm. Cassie snuggled in.

"You shouldn't be. You have a good chance of placing. You never mentioned the prizes."

Cassie wished she were as certain as Luke about her chances, but his optimism always had been contagious. Although she considered herself to be a person who looked for the positive in life, Luke had a way of drawing it out of her naturally. She loved that about him. "First prize is an endorsement from the Chamber. The second is a designated stop with the Door County Bus Tour for a year."

Luke whistled, bringing a smile to Cassie's lips. She liked this new habit of his. It was cute.

"I admire you for entering. It takes courage. One of those prizes could easily put the café on the map."

"Thanks, Luke." Cassie had long since picked up on Luke's support. The way he'd sneak her a smile from his seat at the counter at the café, or how much he told her he'd enjoyed the scone of the day. Lately, they started brainstorming on different variations for the muffins and what coffee blend would be the best compliment. In turn, she shared her accounting software and helped him select paint colors for the clinic's walls.

That was nice too, Cassie thought.

They turned the corner to find a smaller group than the one they left behind. The Chamber's director, Mr. Holland, spoke into the microphone.

"Ladies and gentlemen, thank you for coming today. We had some very impressive entrants in the competition this year, and we'd like to begin with our retail industry."

There were ten categories to get through and Cassie had no idea where cafés fell on the list. She had to ask. "Are you certain you want to stay? This could take a while."

Luke gave her a warm smile. "I'm sure."

Cassie breathed a sigh of relief. She wanted him to stay. She stepped a little closer to Luke. "Thanks, friend."

His eyes crinkled at the corners with his smile. He bumped her shoulder. "You got it, friend."

Over the next thirty minutes, Mr. Holland made his way down the list of contestants. "And our second-place winner is Cassie Hamilton's Perfect Cup Café."

She'd almost missed it! Cassie's smile, as big as a full moon, beamed into the crowd.

Luke grabbed her and pulled her into a hug. "You won second prize!"

Cassie hugged him back. "I can't believe this! I thought I'd blown it."

Luke gave her a gentle shove. "Well get on up there. Everyone's waiting for you."

Mrs. Hall was the first to shake Cassie's hand. "Cassie, you might not have known this, but I went along with Mrs. Ellis to get her picture with Ruby."

"I...didn't know." She discovered the picture on the photo board but had no idea Mrs. Hall had gone along on that visit. Had her heart softened for Ruby?

As if she'd read her mind, Mrs. Hall said, "No, I didn't hold Ruby, but I was there."

Cassie understood, grateful for the kindness the older woman extended her. She accepted her award and ribbon and made sure to make eye contact with each of the committee members. "Thank you so very much."

"We hope this helps you, dear," Mrs. Ellis chimed in.

Cassie was certain it would. She retraced her steps from the presentation area and searched for the man who pulled her into his arms. A hug that felt delicious and warm and safe.

Chapter 9

A few days later, Luke drove to the dance studio where he planned to meet Cassie for their last dance lesson. His mind reeled back to the festival. She'd won second place in the contest. Luke smiled, hoping a stop on the Door County Bus Tours would help her café over the winter. If he were planning to stick around, maybe he'd suggest a cross-marketing arrangement with her café and the clinic.

Luke's mind began to race, *maybe immunizations and a cup of brew* or *get a groom get a cup of java.* He laughed imagining Cassie's response to the idea. She wouldn't quit trying to find ways to save her café. He knew there was one common characteristic within the Hamilton family, and it was the drive toward success. They wouldn't quit. As he approached a red light, he peered into the rearview mirror. *Does she think I'm a quitter for not taking over the vet clinic?* He pushed the idea of Cassie's dissatisfaction to the corner of his mind. It didn't sit well there either.

Luke turned off one of his favorite country songs that played on the radio. He drove the rest of the way in silence, grappling with all that had happened to him since his return to the area. The most surprising of all was the undeniable pull toward Cass. He needed to keep in mind the plans he carefully carved out for the rest of his life. Falling for his best friend's sister wasn't one of them.

He pulled into the studio's parking lot, grabbed his dancing shoes, and headed into the building. About a dozen couples lined the walls and waited for the class to begin. Conrad gave him a nod from across the room and a "you're late" look. Luke held back a groan. Was the man always on watch over his baby sister?

Luke scanned the room and found Cassie seated at one of the tables. She struggled with one of the straps of her blue velvet dance shoes. He walked toward her. "You need some help with that?"

Cassie lifted her head. Lazy curls fell across her shoulders, a much softer look than her work day. "It's always a little awkward with this one."

Luke lowered himself in front of her and rested his weight on one knee. He gave her a wink. "Let's take a look." The heel of her small foot fit easily into the palm of his hand. He slipped the tiny strap through the metal fastener and then smiled up at her. "All set."

She smiled back, off-balancing him for a second. "I can't believe the wedding's next weekend. I guess this means our dance lessons will come to an end."

Luke's heart took a hit. He'd enjoyed the last couple of weeks and the simple moves of a country two-step with Cassie in his arms. He didn't want it to end. "Maybe we could keep taking the lessons." The words fell out of his mouth before he had time to measure their consequences. Didn't he just remind himself of his plans a moment ago?

"You mean after the wedding?"

Luke saw the question in her eyes and heard the lift in her voice. He couldn't help himself. The word slipped from his lips so easily. "Yup."

Cassie's face lit up at the same time the glitter ball overhead started spinning.

He saw the hope in her eyes. He wanted to tell her how pretty she looked tonight but now struggled to find the words. A moment ago, he couldn't keep from suggesting more classes, and now he was tongue-tied? He got to his feet and scanned the room. He had to get his head on straight and his thoughts in the right direction. *What are you doing? Cassie's off-limits, remember? She's your friend's sister, remember? And you're not sticking around, remember?*

"I'm ready." Cassie robbed Luke of time to figure out his next move. She extended her hand in his direction.

That's when everyone else in the room faded away.

She looked so perfect, dressed in a soft cream-colored top and a wispy, pink skirt made for dancing. There was no one prettier in the room. But it was her radiating smile that was making it hard for him to breathe. It said, "We're in this together."

Luke liked that feeling. It was new and foreign and filled him with a contentment he'd never known. To have someone by his side whom he knew he could count on, even in a silly dance competition. Luke wrapped his fingers around hers. *Perfect fit.*

"Let's do it."

Chapter 10

The next morning, Luke waited for an explanation of why his uncle had asked to meet him in the office an hour before they opened. It meant skipping his regular morning stop at the cafe, so he hoped it was important. His intuition told him his uncle found a buyer for the clinic.

Uncle Russ cleared his throat. "I hope what I have to tell you, comes as a welcomed surprise."

Is he kidding? This was exactly what Luke wanted to happen. And the timing couldn't have been better. After meeting with a commercial real estate agent, a couple of weeks ago, Luke tackled the short list of repairs that had to be done before he could list the property. The only job left was the drywall repair in examining room three. A coat of fresh paint throughout the clinic and the delivery of new furniture had Luke counting on a quick sale.

"I need you to be open-minded." Uncle Russ rubbed at the worry lines etching his forehead.

Luke threw up his hands. He'd play along with the surprise, though he didn't understand his uncle's concern. "I'm as open-minded as they come."

"It's about my visit to Doc Wagner's yesterday."

Luke's smile faded. *Huh? What does this have to do with the buyer that came forward?*

Uncle Russ pulled out a chair and motioned Luke to join him. "Doc told me that my arthritis is now in my back. That's why I'm having trouble sleeping and getting out of bed in the morning. He gave me two choices to consider. I can start cortisone injection therapy or think about heading south over the winter. He said many of his patients with arthritis find the warmer weather helpful."

Luke slid his hand through his thick hair. His uncle hated doctoring. "How do you feel about both options?" Luke could have guessed the answer but waited for his uncle's response. The bottom line was that Luke wanted whatever was best for him.

Uncle Russ's cheeks colored red. "Even though I'm a vet, you remember how much I hated giving shots?"

Luke grinned, wishing he could lighten the moment. He could see easily enough that his uncle was struggling. "You bet I do. It's the reason I got as much practice as I did."

"I hate getting them even more."

Luke chuckled but spotted the sheepish look on his Uncle Russ's face. "Are you still opting out of the flu shot every year?"

Russ snorted a chuckle. "An old dog like me doesn't need a flu shot."

"I think it's meant for your age category, but go on." The last image that came to Luke's mind when thinking of his uncle was that of an elderly man. Despite his arthritis, he still managed to play nine holes of golf in a men's league every summer. Luke suspected more for the camaraderie than the sport.

His uncle rubbed his chin. "With everything we've got going on here with the clinic. I told Doc I'd have to talk this over with you before making a decision."

"You're giving the idea of going south some thought then?"

Uncle Russ shrugged. "That depends on you."

Luke swallowed hard. This was the last thing he expected. He forced an easy smile on his face not wanting to make this any harder for his uncle than it already was. "Are we talking about this winter? The one right around the corner?"

Russ worked out a cramp in his hand with his thumb. "Doc mentioned the sooner I leave, the better for my bones."

The hope in his uncle's voice softened Luke's heart. He'd worked a forty-year career in veterinary medicine and had built a reputation that was rock solid.

His uncle winced. "I know you've got your heart set on that big outfit in Minnesota."

"Don't worry about that. I'll work things out on my end if that's what you want to do. It's why I'm here."

His uncle's worried face changed. "Really? Because Cathy has been talking about this place down in Florida. Some fifty-five-and-up community. And she enjoys ballroom dancing just like your Aunt Isabella did. She says they even have therapeutic pools down there."

Luke remembered his aunt and uncle dancing in his younger years. After his aunt's death, the pastime fell to the wayside. He stood a bit dumbfounded now by the notion of someone else in his uncle's life. "Cathy?"

Russ seemed amused. "Lila's aunt."

"Ah, yes. Lila's Aunt Cathy." Luke remembered how Cathy's eyes lit up at the mention of his uncle's name at Bobby's party. Now that he was thinking about it, Luke remembered his uncle mentioning something about Cathy and heading south in an earlier conversation.

"We've been…well…seeing each other." His uncle fidgeted in his seat.

Luke began to move the pieces into place. *He's dating?* "So, you two are thinking of maybe traveling down there together?"

His uncle's face lit up like those of a much younger man. "Separate units, of course, but she's been encouraging me along those lines. Yes."

Luke didn't stop his lips from curling into a smile.

"Why are you looking at me like that? I may be an old dog but not a dead one." His eyebrows waggled. "Can we make this work, Luke?"

Luke smiled at the thought. His uncle had been alone for so long. "You bet we can. I'll finish what's left of the repairs and get the place on the market. And don't worry about the real estate closing. That's all done over the computer. You don't have to be here for that."

Russ moved toward Luke, pulled him close, and squeezed him tight as he used to when he was a kid.

Luke sensed the relief fall from his uncle's shoulders in the embrace. The robust strong frame he'd expected had changed. Visions of his uncle lifting a ninety-pound shepherd onto the examining table flooded in. Luke's throat drew tight. Why hadn't he noticed his uncle's decline before this? *Worrying about myself, that's why.*

The scent of tobacco from his morning pipe lingered in his uncle's hair. The end of an era was near. Luke squeezed back a hug. He hadn't expected the fallout from his decision not to take over the clinic to have such an effect on him. This was tougher than he'd imagined it would be.

His uncle pulled back and looked him straight in the eyes. "I can't tell you how much this means to me." His uncle moved his head from side to side. "Are you one hundred percent sure you don't want the practice? It might not be as exciting as what you're going after, but it's a good life, Luke. A happy life. It'll give you a sense of accomplishment and purpose off the charts."

How could Luke explain that deep down he wasn't cut from the same cloth but from his dad's? A man who never held a job for more than a couple of years at a time. *I did the same thing during high school and college.* Looking back, he wasn't proud of the choices he'd made, or how he handled ditching one job and picking up another. Many times, those decisions were made on nothing more than a whim or a dare from his buddies. He carried a good amount of shame on his back because of those decisions, but he couldn't change now. It was too late. If not for his uncle's argument to his parents that he needed the experience of holding a steady job, he never would've worked at the clinic or discovered his life's work.

Looking into his eyes, Luke was certain he wasn't the man his uncle thought he was. He searched for the right words to answer his question. "I, uh…"

His uncle's natural talent and finesse to fill in the awkward gaps in life sprung to life. "Thank you, my boy, for helping me out when I needed it."

Luke swallowed the lump in his throat, wishing it could be different. "You bet. Why don't you give Cathy a call and get the ball rolling."

Russ's face lit up. "Good idea."

Luke watched him walk down the hall with a lighter step. No doubt he'd call Cathy right away with the good news. This would cause another delay in Luke's plans. He tipped his head and stared at the ceiling. *The interview appointment.* With most of the repairs completed, Luke had foolishly moved forward and arranged for the final interview appointment with PetsAmerica last week. It never occurred to him to discuss it with his uncle before making the call. Now, he'd have to cancel that appointment. Again.

Luke wished for one of the racehorses he used to groom. He'd climb aboard right about now and ride and ride and ride. But that wasn't an option.

He tipped his head to the ceiling and prayed to be a better man than he knew he was. *This is nothing more than a setback, that's all.*

Chapter 11

Cassie's frustration grew. Seated behind a sewing machine in Sally McPherson's hobby haven room, she lunged for the seam ripper. Why was making a quilted square so difficult? If she could match up the quilt squares correctly before sewing them together that would help. It didn't sound hard when given the instruction, but talking with Sally while working on her table runner had proven otherwise.

Sally smiled. "You'll need more than one go at this to get it down. Most people will tell you quilting is an art. It takes a ton of patience, as you already know."

Cassie drew a breath. "What you mean to say is that it can bring you to your knees."

Sally's chuckle filled the room. She tapped, tapped, tapped the foot control of her sewing machine, and it began its purr down the final seam of her project.

Cassie had dabbled in a few simple quilting projects, but when she spotted the intricate table runners at Sally's craft booth at the Harvest Moon Festival, she'd convinced herself she could handle the project. The bold fabric colors, the curve in design, and the lacey edges had impressed her. When Sally McPherson suggested they'd make a beautiful enhancement for the café, Cassie jumped at the suggestion to make them together. But now, two hours into the project, and not one completed, Cassie wasn't sure she liked the idea at all.

The front door on the first floor opened with a bang, rattling the framed pictures on the staircase wall, interrupting Cassie's next complaint.

"Sally, Sally honey, come quick. It's Lulu." Charlie McPherson's voice rang loud through the house like the chimes on their grandfather clock in the hallway.

Cassie followed Sally's quick steps out of the room and down the stairs to find an exhausted Charlie, waiting for them. His hand rested on the newel. Labored breaths told Cassie he'd probably jogged up from the barn to the house.

"I think it's getting close for Lulu. You'd better call Doc Hunter."

Sally untied the sewing apron she wore with her projects and draped it over the banister. "Already did. I could see it coming early this morning when I saw her nesting in the barn. Luke's on his way."

Charlie straightened his bent-over frame and threw his shoulders back. "Luke? Why not Russ? Lulu isn't going to want a stranger to get her through this."

Cassie bit her lower lip, picking up on the irritation in Charlie's voice. This would certainly be an uncomfortable situation if Charlie didn't want Luke as Lulu's doctor. It was the dog's first litter.

"Honey, Luke's no stranger to Lulu. He was just here visiting. Remember? He bought the Noah's ark train set for Conrad's little boy."

Charlie wiped the perspiration from his brow with

a red bandana kerchief. "Yes, I remember. I'd still rather have Russ." Charlie's agitation grew, despite his wife's argument.

Sally smiled, and Charlie's tense shoulders relaxed. "I know, but Russ is retiring. Luke's taking over."

Charlie's mouth gaped. "Is that what Russ told you? He's retiring?"

Cassie pursed her lips. It wasn't her place to tell the McPhersons that Luke planned to sell the clinic. She'd leave that for him to explain. But this is a good example of what she tried explaining to Luke when he first mentioned selling the practice. Folks wouldn't take to that kind of change well.

Sally's mouth turned downward. "You know Russ has been hurting for a long time with that awful arthritis. Let's be thankful we've got a young man to take over." Sally's gaze moved from her husband to the large picture window in the next room. "That must be him now."

Cassie lifted on tiptoes to get a look at the oncoming vehicle. "By the way he's driving, it doesn't look like he wasted any time getting here." She grabbed her jacket and followed Charlie and Sally down the front walk to meet Luke.

Ruby came running toward her from the open field. Cassie bent to greet her. "Come here, girl."

Luke's Jeep skidded to a stop, scattering the loose gravel. The engine went quiet, and the vehicle door opened. "Hello, folks. I understand it's time for your Lulu to have her puppies. Uncle Russ has filled me in on all the details." Luke's warm smile landed on Cassie while Ruby bolted toward him.

"Hello, Cassie, I didn't know *you'd* be here." Luke ruffled Ruby's head. "How's my girl doing today?"

Sally gave Cassie an elbow jab. "Told you," she sang.

Cassie shushed Sally's comment with wide, scolding eyes. "I'm here working on table runners for the café. Sally's a big help," she told Luke.

Charlie stepped forward. "I understand you're taking over for Russ now?" His pointed question was directed at Luke. His tone was down to business.

Luke raised a hand, and Cassie figured he was about to fill the McPhersons in on his plans. "I'd like to…" he started.

Charlie began the trek to the barn. "You got everything you need, Son?" he asked over his shoulder. The irritation in his voice was hard to miss.

Luke must have refocused in a blink because he patted his doctor's bag. "I've got everything right here. Sally, can you grab a stack of towels, a laundry basket, and a heating pad if you have one? We'll need to get the pups out of mom's way as soon as they're born but keep them close where she can see them."

"You got it," Sally retraced her steps back to the house to collect the items while Luke and Charlie headed to the barn.

Cassie decided she'd be of more use to Luke than to Sally and followed behind the men, Ruby on her heels.

After stepping into the barn, Luke removed his jacket. He placed it on a nearby hay bale along with his bag. Cassie followed his lead. She stood next to him and observed Luke as much as she did Lulu.

For what seemed like forever, Luke simply

observed Lulu. Then he bent down close and allowed her to sniff his scent. He murmured something Cassie couldn't quite make out. Whatever it was had a calming effect on the dog. Her panting eased as she turned her head and looked at him as if giving Luke her consent to treat her. Luke's gentle approach to an animal in distress had always impressed Cassie. It hadn't surprised her to see it first-hand with Lulu.

"Can you hand me my bag, Cassie?"

"Yes, of course." Cassie slipped into the shoes of his veterinary assistant and passed his bag to him.

Luke gave Charlie a firm look. "She knows what to do. The whelping process is natural for her, but now she understands I'm a friend."

Sally entered the barn, her arms full of the supplies Luke had asked her for. "I thought something was up yesterday." She placed the laundry basket filled with towels and a blue heating blanket near Cassie's feet. "She didn't eat a thing and that's not like our Lulu. That's when I called Russ." She plugged in the electric blanket with the help of an extension cord and set the dial to low.

"She's been restless more than usual too. Keeps pawing at her bed. She goes in, comes out, and goes back in again. Makes no sense," Charlie added. His voice was evident with concern for the dog who was always at his side.

Luke spoke over his shoulder toward Charlie. "Sounds like she's been getting ready for her pups. Let's take a look and see how things are progressing."

Cassie bent down alongside Luke and ran her hand down Lulu's head. "It's okay Lulu," she repeated over and over. She spoke in the same soft tones as Luke had used a moment ago but wished she'd heard what he'd said to the animal that calmed her.

"Contractions are strong now. Here we go." Luke handed Cassie a pair of gloves and slipped on a pair of his own. "We should see our first pup real soon."

Cassie's eyes widened. *What a thrill!* She'd been present when dogs gave birth in the past, but today it held more meaning at Luke's side. Like the decisions they made together for the café and the clinic, they were a team once again and would work together to see this through.

Over the next hour, Lulu's contractions came and went as she delivered six German shepherd mixed puppies. One cuter than the last.

Cassie assumed it was over until Luke said, "We've got a problem here. The last one appears either stuck or turned in the wrong direction."

"Oh, no," Sally moaned, "our poor Lulu."

Cassie spotted something. "Is that the tail?"

Luke turned to her. "Good observation. I'll make a vet assistant out of you yet."

His comment brought a smile to Cassie's lips and eased some of the tension in the room. Would that be a real possibility if Luke stayed? The thought made her heart skip a beat. What an unexpected turn God would make in her life if that happened.

"Cassie, I'd like you to place the flat of your hands right here and apply a small amount of pressure."

Cassie followed Luke's instructions. Placing her hands on Lulu's midsection, she pressed down until he gave her the nod to stop.

Luke leaned in on bent knees. "I'm going to help Lulu by pulling down on the tail and trying to reach one of the back legs."

It all happened in a blink. A black and white little fur baby slid into Luke's open hands.

"There she is," Luke grinned.

Charlie stepped forward and patted Luke's back in rapid successive beats. "Would you look at that," he marveled, "just look at that."

Luke placed the last of the pups close to Lulu's head who nuzzled the runt of the litter close for her first bath. Soon she wiggled free from her mother's examination and started nursing.

Sally yelled, "Hooray, Lulu. Good girl."

Cassie's gaze flew to Luke now sitting back on his heels doing his best to catch his breath. Relief and praise washed over his face. "It's been a while since I delivered a litter of pups." He removed the gloves from his hands.

"Now you tell us?" Charlie chuckled.

"You did it," Cassie said. This was the reason she was here today. Not to work on her quilt squares to make runners for the cafe, but to be at Luke's side where she was needed the most. Was it impulse, excitement, or both when she wrapped her arms around Luke's neck and hugged him?

"I couldn't have done it without you," he murmured in her ear, holding her tight.

It was Charlie's question that broke the spell between them, and that's when Cassie caught Sally's wink.

"What do we do now?" Charlie asked.

For the next hour, Luke explained what to expect from mom and pups. It wasn't until they reached the Jeep that Charlie stuck his hand out in Luke's direction.

Cassie turned toward Sally and stroked Ruby's head. She had a good idea of what was coming next and wanted to give the two men some privacy.

"I owe you a big apology, young man," Charlie stuffed his hands in his pockets. He tucked his chin under the collar of his coat.

Luke tipped his head. "For what?"

Was it possible Luke never picked up on Charlie's adverse attitude when he arrived? It wouldn't surprise Cassie if he didn't. Luke didn't judge people for their missteps. It was one of his attributes she'd always admired and wished she had a big dose of herself.

"I underestimated you. You came through just like Russ would have. That'll never happen again." Charlie offered his hand.

Cassie caught the look on Luke's face as the two men shook hands. Charlie's apology had touched Luke somewhere deep inside of him. Was he surprised at Charlie's words? Whatever happened here this afternoon was bigger than Lulu giving birth, much bigger.

The moment was gone as quickly as it had appeared when Luke returned an easy smile. "Be sure to check on Lulu and the pups every couple of hours. It's important they continue nursing and be kept warm. Call if you need me."

"You bet I will. I plan to bunk out there tonight."

"What?" Sally's question sounded more like a demand. "You most certainly will not, Mr. McPherson. You'll catch a cold that'll turn into bronchitis. It happens every year and you've got a heart…"

Charlie bumped his shoulder against Luke's and ducked his head, blocking his wife's protest. "She wouldn't know what to do if she didn't worry about me."

Luke chuckled as he placed his bag in the back seat, got into the jeep, and started up the engine.

"I'll watch over our Lulu. Thanks, Doc." Charlie waved.

Luke returned the wave as he drove off, and Cassie was satisfied that it all went well. Luke had handled an uncomfortable situation beautifully, whether he realized it or not.

She watched Luke's vehicle cover the last of the stone-covered driveway. She reflected on what just happened here. That look in Luke's eyes was so telling. Was Luke finally getting it? She hoped so. This small community in the heart of Door County needed his holistic expertise with animals. She wanted to give herself the freedom to need him too, but she couldn't, not yet.

Chapter 12

On Saturday morning, after a home visit for a persnickety cat at Ms. Murphy's, Luke picked up the items he'd ordered from the vet supply store and headed over to Taylor Farms. Earlier, Chet had asked him to stop by and mentioned a wedding gift for Andrea. The idea intrigued Luke. How did *he* factor into a wedding present for Chet's soon-to-be wife? He also wanted to see how his friend was holding up with only a matter of hours before his wedding.

His phone buzzed interrupting his scattered thoughts. Luke pulled over to the side of the road. PetsAmerica flashed across the screen.

Luke hit the steering wheel with the palms of his hands. Were they calling to tell him they'd hired someone else and his interview appointment was canceled? As disappointed as he'd be, he couldn't blame them. He'd canceled on them twice. He shook his head in frustration. In both situations, he'd been caught between a rock and a hard place.

The phone buzzed again. He took a deep breath trying to prepare himself for the bad news and answered the call.

"Dr. Hunter, are you there?" A pleasant voice

asked.

Light snow fell on Luke's windshield. He switched off the wipers. "Yes, this is he."

"This is Sasha calling from PetsAmerica. Please hold for Mr. Schultz."

"Yes, of course." Luke half-expected a call from the HR director but wished it had come at a better time.

A recorded infomercial informed Luke of the groom specials and upcoming immunization schedule offered at the store.

"Luke, Ernie Schultz here."

"Hello, Mr. Schultz."

"Just want to confirm your interview appointment next week."

"Of course. It's on my schedule." Luke replied, thankful he'd pulled off the highway and could give the call his full attention. This must mean he was still in the running for the job. He did his best to slow his racing heart. "I plan to leave a day early so the weather doesn't interfere with travel." He didn't have the leeway for one more interruption.

"Good to hear. I don't have to tell you that this will be your last opportunity. To be honest, I would've passed you by, but you've got someone in your corner giving you a high recommendation."

Luke's shoulders hit the back of the seat. *Who could that be?* "I appreciate it, Mr. Schultz. I'll be there."

"Very good. I look forward to meeting you in person."

After the call, Luke thanked God for the second chance, then reminded himself that it was a third chance to land this job. He reached for the to-go cup of coffee that had grown cold and took a long swig. Peering into the cup, he swirled the brown liquid and winced. This was a far cry from Cassie's blend of the day. Funny how his mind went straight back to her. The truth was, he couldn't wait to see her tonight at Chet's wedding. What was it about her that made him feel so content? If that's how she was with everyone, it was a true gift. Luke had never been as comfortable with a woman as he was with her.

He pulled back into the traffic and resumed his journey to Chet's. Instead of listening to the radio his mind drifted. From the moment he'd passed his veterinary exam and received his license, his number one priority was joining PetsAmerica. He and his parents agreed it would give him the chance to see the country with a new contract every three years. 'You're just like your father but in a good way,' he heard his mother's voice in his head, which only reaffirmed his decision to pursue the job.

Cassie's smile floated across his mind. He'd surely miss it. Luke exhaled an agitated breath. That kind of thinking wasn't going to help. *Keep your priorities straight, Hunter.*

He turned into the long drive leading to Chet's farm. He'd told Luke to head over to the barn. Not what Luke had expected to hear. The wedding was later this afternoon. Shouldn't Chet be getting ready for the big day?

Minutes later, Luke stood in the center of the building overwhelmed as he took in the details. He'd never seen anything quite like it. Streamers and balloons hung from the rafters. *Wow! How did they manage that?* Flowers, polished silver, and tables set for dinner all transformed the barn into a wedding hall.

The pinging of a hammer striking wood caught Luke's attention. He followed the racket to the back of the room. He found Chet on his back hammering a set of stairs to a small platform.

"This is what a man does on the day he gets married?" Luke couldn't believe his eyes.

Chet removed the nail clenched between his teeth. "It is when you're the guy in charge." He rolled to his side and got to his feet. "Thanks for coming out."

"No problem. I had a home visit and a run down to Sturgeon Bay to pick up a few supplies for the clinic. You're right on the way home. What's up?"

Chet leaned against a support beam and slid one boot on top of the other. If he were anxious about getting married, it didn't show. The calm look on his face gave Luke the impression it was an ordinary day.

"Andrea's heart is set on a Bassett hound puppy. I was hoping you could find one for her."

"Ah," Luke smiled. Although Chet's attributes were many, thoughtfulness had never made the list. The love of a good woman had definitely changed him. "That's probably one of the most unique wedding gifts I've ever heard of."

Chet gave a tilt of his head. "Here's the problem."

Luke picked up on Chet's apprehension. He wanted to make it easier for his friend, but he had no clue what was coming next.

"I'm taking Andrea to France for our honeymoon."

Luke whistled. Europe was on his own places to see list, especially Paris. Now he understood where this conversation was headed.

"If you could locate the dog Andrea wants so bad

and take him under your wing until we get back, I'd owe you."

Oh boy. Luke did a quick calculation. He couldn't allow another delay to interfere with the PetsAmerica interview coming up. He stalled.

"You haven't sold the clinic yet, have you?"

Luke shook his head. Chet was assuming he had to stick around until the clinic was sold. "It's listed, but no offers, yet. I'm still finishing up the renovations."

"So, you're planning on sticking around?"

Bingo. Just as I thought. Chet was unaware that Luke didn't need the clinic to be sold to take off. With the help of the Internet, all the realtor needed was a lockbox and an email to facilitate the sale and closing.

Luke needed a minute to think Chet's request through. He wanted to help his buddy out, but he wanted that interview to go through just as badly. He needed to buy himself a little time. "This is quite the layout you've got here."

"I've been working on it for the last month to get all the details Andrea wanted." Chet scanned the room. "Hope she loves it."

"No doubt, she will." Luke smiled at the level of contentment on his friend's face. *Amazing.* Another example of how love must have softened Chet's tough exterior and mended the wounds he'd carried for so long.

Chet threw the hammer and nail into a toolbox and secured the lid. "So, what do you think? Can you help me out?"

There was no way Luke would let Chet down. He'd figure it out. "I'll make some calls. You want a male or female?"

"Better make it a female. Andrea might want Lucy to have her own litter one day."

"Lucy?" Luke shook his head. "She's already picked out a name?"

A wide smile spread across Chet's face. "Like I said. Andrea's heart is set on it."

It was obvious to Luke that Chet had no intention of letting Andrea down. "I'm on it."

"Thanks, man. I knew I could count on you."

Luke liked the sound of Chet's confidence in him. He was relying on him to come through. He had heard similar comments from the customers of the clinic or after one of his house calls that were now becoming more common. But coming from a friend had a different effect on him.

"Next time you need a favor, I'm there." Chet grabbed his jacket from the floor.

Luke headed for the door. "Don't worry about it, that's what friends are for."

"I'll walk out with you. It's almost time for me to get cleaned up and marry the love of my life. I brought all the stuff I'd need here to the inn."

"Good idea. Saves you a trip back to your place."

They walked in comfortable silence down the driveway until Luke turned to Chet. "Andrea seems like a great girl."

"I got lucky."

Cassie would tell him she didn't believe in luck.

"I have to admit, I never saw it coming."

Luke frowned. "What?"

Chet shrugged. "Love. But it was so easy with Andrea. She saw all the good, bad, and ugly in me and loved me anyway. When she went back to New York, it felt as if the bottom of my life fell out. I knew then I didn't want to live another day without her. I needed her in my life."

As they continued their path, Luke wrestled with an unfamiliar response to Chet's candidness. *Envy?* Nah. He wasn't jealous of his friend for falling in love. He was happy for the guy as much as he was for Conrad and Lila, another love story for the books.

Before long, they made their way to the top of the drive. This is where Chet would turn toward the main house and Luke toward his Jeep.

Chet gave him a serious look. "I've been in your shoes."

Huh? Luke didn't follow. "How do you mean?"

"Running from the idea of needing someone. If it weren't for Conrad and my dad, and God who worked a flat-out miracle with that pride of mine, I wouldn't be getting married today. I was bullheaded and stubborn."

Luke gave Chet's shoulder a fist bump. "I'm happy for you, but that has nothing to do with me."

Chet threw him a stern look. "I know you always had a thing for Cassie, even when she was hiding behind Conrad."

"I...ah...um..." Luke heard himself blubbering. *What's wrong with my lips?* "I haven't fallen for anybody, especially not for one of my best friend's sisters."

Chet cocked his head. "Why not your best friend's sister?"

Luke scoffed. He could diagnose an animal's distress in a heartbeat, but when Cassie came into the picture, he froze.

"You got something in that stubborn head of yours

that tells you you're not good enough? 'Cause, I've been there too."

Luke swallowed. Hard. He didn't *think* he wasn't good enough for Cassie. He knew he wasn't. Not with his DNA. Like it or not, he was a rambling man just like his dad. He'd been told that enough all of his life. He was tired of pretending it wasn't true. Besides, Cassie deserved better than that. She deserved the best a man could offer. One who wanted the same things she did like making roots in a community, having family close by, and a business she could call her own.

"We all grew up with an idea for our future, but that doesn't mean we can't change our minds if a better version of our life comes along. Because that *better* might be our destiny. Just think about it."

"Says the man about to step off the cliff," Luke chuckled. He didn't want to entertain an alternate plan for his future, despite his growing feelings for Cassie. His future was set, and Luke was certain it would suit him to a tee.

Chet chuckled. "I remember grilling Conrad with the same words we said we'd use on each other on our wedding days. I'll see you later. I'll be the guy waiting up front grinning from ear to ear." He turned toward the main house and started his trek up another hill.

"See you in a few." Luke picked up the pace to his Jeep, and a few minutes later, started up the engine and headed home. He considered his friend's advice. But then he reminded himself of the truth that sat deep inside of him.

Luke's shoulders caved as he forced his focus back to where it belonged. He had to do everything in his power to land that job. As hard as it might be, he needed to start distancing himself from the woman he loved spending time with.

A few hours later, after a quick shower, a shave, and getting dressed, Luke intended to head straight over to the wedding but a phone call changed his plans. Sooner than expected, the drywall repair job in examining room three was finished. Luke slipped his watch over his wrist and noted the time. He could swing by the clinic and set up a pair of old reliable space heaters he'd spotted in the storage closet last week. He was surprised his uncle still had them. That would help speed up the new drywall drying time, so the painters could get started next week.

The sooner he could move this project along, the better.

Chapter 13

Cassie was skeptical to attend a wedding held in a renovated hay barn, but her eyes grew wide in disbelief when she stepped inside. Now dressed out with flowers in russet reds, vibrant oranges, and coffee-colored browns, the old pole barn at Taylor Farms had truly been transformed. The scent of hay was near but out of eyeshot. Her heels clicked on the wooden-planked floor installed for this special day.

She strolled past the buffet tables admiring the layout and almost ran smack-dab into Lila. The matron-of-honor wore a long chiffon dress, in a rich pumpkin color while her tousled hair was styled in a lazy updo. She smiled at Cassie.

"I can't believe my eyes. This is stunning."

Lila's head moved slowly from side to side. "Chet has worked so hard creating a wonderful venue for special events, hasn't he?" She said as she cast another glance around the generous space.

"Amazing. I thought the retirement party last year for his father was impressive, but this takes your breath away." Cassie scanned the room, looking for Luke. "I love weddings, don't you?"

Lila gave her a sideways glance and grinned,

leading Cassie to suspect if she'd read her mind again. She seemed to have a knack for that. "If you're looking for Luke, he's saved you a chair. Said it was for his plus-one date."

"I wasn't looking for Luke." Cassie frowned and Lila chuckled. "Plus-one and date don't belong in the same sentence." She'd be smart to remind herself that Luke's plans for the future did not include her, despite how her feelings continued to grow for him.

Lila tapped her slender finger against her cheek. "Now you sound like an editor."

Cassie removed her shawl from her shoulders and draped it over her arm. "Are you ready for the dance contest tonight?"

Lila moved her feet into a box pattern. "We've been practicing every night for the last two weeks."

Cassie lifted her eyebrows. "Looks like you're ready. Luke plans to add what he calls 'our special move' at the end of our dance. Any idea when the competition starts?"

Lila joined Cassie as she continued her stroll past the tables, admiring the layout. "You know Chet. It'll be a mystery until he pulls it out of his hat."

"He and Andrea seem like such a perfect match. Just like you and Conrad. I can't wait to see her in her wedding dress."

"They're perfect for each other. A blend of rugged and refined just like the wedding. Did you notice the cello player and violinist over there?" Lila motioned to the seated area.

Cassie's gaze shifted from finally spotting the hay bales to the shimmery streamers overhead. The musicians were directly behind the small platform stage. "Oh, my. What an elegant touch for a barn wedding. You're right, it's a perfect example of Chet and Andrea."

Lila bent to whisper in Cassie's ear. "I'd wish you good luck with your dance, but if Conrad found out, he might disown me as his partner." Cassie giggled and Lila joined in.

"I don't think Luke and I will be much of a threat. In the end, Luke emphasized that having fun was more important than winning a prize."

Lila rolled her eyes. "Typical Luke, always the gentleman."

Cassie couldn't disagree with that statement.

The music grew louder causing a stir as the guests took their seats on the pretty white linen chairs with oversized bows.

"I'd better scoot and get in my position," Lila said.

"And I'd better find Luke. Good luck, not that you need it."

As the guests filed into the rows of chairs, Cassie rose on tip-toes in search of Luke. She'd seen him only a moment ago. He wore a smart navy-blue suit that gave him a dashing look. As everyone else scrambled for the perfect seat, she'd lost sight of him. The music heightened along with her heart. *Is that him?* Her breath caught as she stared straight ahead. That was him all right. He stood three rows from center stage with his arms around a pretty brunette.

Cassie's stomach dropped as the blood drained from her face.

~

Luke picked up on Cassie's bold stride moving toward him. He saw the question in her eyes. Was he in trouble? Knowing Cassie as he did, she wouldn't hold back from giving it to him, formal setting or no formal setting. She spoke her mind, and she didn't hold back on her opinions. He'd always admired that about her.

Until now.

As Cassie approached, the woman in his arms fell from his embrace and turned around.

"Cassie, it's so good to see you," she said.

Cassie's feet slowed. Her face softened when she recognized their dance instructor Alaina Bell. Luke tilted his head, confused. Then it hit him. She hadn't been able to tell who was in his embrace. Which meant…what?

Cassie gently squeezed Alaina's fingers in her hand. "I had no idea we'd see you here tonight."

Alaina had been invaluable to them in the weeks they prepared for their song on the dance floor. The two women smiled at each other until Alaina picked up her velvet blue clutch from the chair. "Andrea and Chet asked that I watch their wedding dance for moral support and to help judge the competition. I was only happy to oblige."

Luke stepped closer to Cassie and placed his hand on the small of her back. She was a knockout in the dress she wore. "You look absolutely lovely tonight, Cass."

"Thank you, Luke."

The music changed. Chet and his brother moved into position on center stage. "Looks like we'd better take our seats," Luke suggested.

"Let's talk later," Alaina said. "Good luck with the competition. You've got this." She gave them both a thumbs up and headed toward her seat.

An hour later, Luke did his best to remember the events of the wedding ceremony. His gaze fell on the beautiful lady sitting next to him. She had every woman in here beaten by a mile, including the bride. Ah, wait a minute. *Where's my head going again?* He was her plus-one date and nothing more. She'd made that clear when this whole idea was launched. He'd be wise to remember that.

Right after the cake cutting and the dessert was served, Luke swiveled around in his seat to the buzz of activity behind him. The buffet tables were being cleared and disassembled. Soon the dance floor would come into view.

He turned to Cassie. "You feel like a little fresh air before the dance begins with your plus-one?"

She returned a look he couldn't quite read but rose from her chair to accompany him outside. "I think we've moved well past this plus-one category, don't you?"

His eyes melted into her deep double browns he'd always loved. Pushing his plans for the future aside, he fought the urge to kiss her. "Yes, I believe we have."

He offered Cassie his arm and led her outside. Noticing her heels, he pulled her close and navigated them onto a grassy area toward a set of outdoor furniture. *I like having her right by my side.*

"I love the improvements Chet has made, don't you?"

Luke's gaze swept over the sea of green grass and majestic trees. This is an ideal place to ride, he thought. "Chet always had a lot of ideas for the farm, but that wild streak in him almost ruined it all."

Cassie seemed to agree. "You're right. He and his

dad had a rough patch to get through, but family is family. It's what's most important in life. Chet admits to learning a powerful lesson from the years he spent in Vegas."

"He always was good at cards. I guess we're all guilty of that indulgence."

"You mean cards? I've never cared for the pastime."

"No. To dream about the roads we could travel in a lifetime."

Cassie draped a shawl around her shoulders, while Luke watched the breeze play with her hair. "I never wanted to be anywhere but here. I guess I'll always be just a small-town girl at heart."

Luke hoped she believed what he was about to tell her. "One with an entrepreneur's spirit, no doubt, just like the rest of your clan."

"Can I be honest?"

He spotted a couple of wicker chairs under a mature oak tree. They faced an open pasture bordered by white rail fencing. *This is the perfect spot.* He gestured to them. As they took a seat, a flock of geese flew past overhead, heading south. "You can tell me anything. I hope you know that by now."

Cassie smiled. At that moment, Luke was forced to face a hard truth. *I could look at that smile forever.*

"It's not the success of the business that drives me like it does for the rest of my family. It's the relationships I have with my customers. Yes, I have to be concerned about the off-season, but it's the little tasks I love the most—like turning over the closed sign to open, starting the coffee pots to perk, the sound of the bell tinkling when one of my customers walks in."

She placed her hand on top of Luke's, sending an army of sparks up his arm. "That includes you now too."

Her admission struck a familiar chord deep inside Luke. He recalled the joy he'd experienced when returning every summer and working at the clinic with his uncle. Before long, pets began to recognize him. Like Cassie, it was the little things he enjoyed the most.

Luke rested his arms on his thighs. "I get it."

"But you don't want that for yourself. Right?"

Cassie's question had Luke drifting in a direction he wasn't prepared for. A movie played in his head. One with him and Cassie working side by side. Where were they in this movie? He couldn't make it out, couldn't dial in that close. But he heard the laughter between them and felt the contentment that settled him. He was happy.

"Luke?"

Luke shook himself out of it. How long had he drifted off in la-la land? He rose to his feet, and Cassie followed his lead. "Hmm?"

Cassie smiled, brushing the incident aside. "It's not important."

He reached out his hand toward her and she laced her fingers between his. "You probably already know this, but I've always had a thing for you."

Her eyes widened, recalling Sally McPherson's comment. She was right after all. As hard as she might try, Cassie couldn't deny the same truth for the man standing in front of her. "It's nice, isn't it, to find someone you're in sync with?"

Luke moved a strand of hair from her face. He heard the warnings in his head and knew he shouldn't do what he was about to do, but he couldn't help himself. He couldn't stop the collision course between what he felt for this woman and his plans for the future. Just once, he told himself.

"I have a good idea what else would be nice for us." He gently pulled her toward him and then bent his head toward hers. The sweet scent of lilacs surrounded him when his eyes met hers. *If she pulls away from me, I'll understand.*

The wispy touch of her fingertips ran down his cheek, causing his heart to hammer against his chest.

When her eyes fluttered closed and her lips parted, he knew.

Ever so softly he brushed his lips against hers in a light kiss. It was just as he imagined. Perfect.

When the kiss ended, her lips curled in a smile. "Oh-oh."

Luke chuckled and then bit the side of his cheek. "Oh-oh is right. You have no idea how long I've been wanting to do that."

"And you have no idea how long I've wanted you to do it," Cassie admitted.

Luke stroked her hair. The silky strands slipped through his fingers like water. He glanced over his shoulder. If Conrad spotted them, he'd have a lot of explaining to do. He'd entrusted him as Cassie's date. Luke wasn't sure if he'd approve of what just happened between them. "As much as I'd rather stay right here, we'd better high-tail it back inside before your big brother comes looking for you. I'm not sure how pleased he'd be with me right now."

Cassie redirected his attention with a light touch. "I'm not worried about Conrad right now." She flashed him a mischievous grin and then leaned in for another kiss. When they broke apart, she peered up at him and then slipped her arm into his. "Now, I'm ready."

Luke felt the grin spread across his face as he led her back toward the barn, dragging a champagne-dizzy state of mind along with him.

Stepping inside, Cassie gasped. "What in the world happened in the short time we were gone?"

Luke scanned the room, watching guests hustle into groups. "Looks like they're setting up for the dance competition. We'd better find out what's going on."

Conrad and Lila strode toward them. "We wondered where you two ran off to," Conrad said.

Luke heard the question in his voice that needed answering.

"We just went out to get a bit of fresh air," Cassie said, calming her overprotective older sibling.

"You need to get your numbers on." Conrad turned to reveal the number 12 pinned to his and Lila's backs. Go over to the registration table. It's across the room, near the band."

"They'll tell you where your group is," Lila said. "We're in the smooth dance category."

"Thanks. Good luck you two." Luke grabbed Cassie's hand and navigated them through a thick crowd of contestants toward the registration table. He had no idea so many guests would be interested in competing. It appeared that Chet and Andrea's idea to spice up the wedding with a dance contest was a big hit.

With their numbers pinned to their backs, Luke and Cassie stood side-by-side waiting for their group to be called out onto the dance floor. Cassie tightened up next to him. He squeezed her hand, hoping to chase away any jitters she might be struggling with. His mind wasn't on winning. Instead, he wanted nothing more than for Cassie to enjoy herself.

The drummer tapped on the cymbals energizing the crowd, drawing their attention. Luke saw Chet walk across the stage and grab the microphone. "Ladies and gentlemen, the fun is about to begin." Chet's voice boomed over the crowd. Andrea stood at her new husband's side. "The dance competition begins right now."

"We're going to start with a waltz. Dancers take the floor," Chet instructed.

"Look," Cassie pointed, "there goes Conrad and Lila."

Luke watched his friend lead Lila to the center of the floor. "It's good they took the middle."

"Oh? Why?"

"The less experienced should always take the middle so they're not in the way of the more experienced dancers. It's a courtesy thing."

"I'm glad you know the rules. I wouldn't want us making any mistakes out there."

Chet reached for her hand. "Don't worry, I'll keep you straight. So, in the end, Conrad and Lila picked a waltz. I'd pick a country ballad every time. The music was always one of the best parts of living in Nashville."

"I think that's Lila's favorite dance."

Chet got it. Conrad would do anything to keep his wife happy, even if it meant entering a dance contest. "Ah, makes sense then."

Cassie drew close and whispered in Luke's ear. "I'm so glad we got back just in time."

He tugged her close. Her shoulder fit snuggly under his. Desire roared through him. He wanted to kiss her again right then and there.

"I can't imagine what was keeping us." Luke grinned, reflecting the smile on her face. He noticed the sparkle in her eyes and the light illuminating the tiny gold flecks.

"Me either. But I hope to have the same problem again very soon."

Luke couldn't have agreed more. "Me too."

Once the waltz had ended, the country-western group was invited to take the floor. Luke's adrenaline soared off the charts. He was ready for this. He turned to Cassie, expecting she'd be as excited as he was. She wasn't. Her feet seemed glued in place. Panic swirled in her eyes. He had to fix this and fast. "We've got our dance down. Muscle memory will kick in. All we have to do now is have fun out there."

Cassie reached for his hand. The color in her cheeks was still pale. "Okay. I'm depending on you to get us through this."

Luke's shoulders straightened. *She needs me.* He gave her an encouraging smile and hoped it wiped away her hesitation. "We can do this," he assured her.

Luke understood the instructions he'd heard earlier at the registration table. The dancers were unaware of what song would be chosen. The only clue they were given was that it'd be a popular country tune. Luke would have to adjust his steps according to the beat and tempo—and it had to be done immediately. Starting the dance offbeat would do them in.

The twang of a guitar started the music, fueling his legs. His feet tapped to the beat, picking up the tempo. He loved the stories behind country music. The one playing now happened to be one of his favorites. The song spoke of a man who'd lost everything important in life because of one wrong decision. *'I was chasing a dream, a silly dream, and on the way to finding it, I lost you.'* He hoped that man would never be him.

Luke took his time as he navigated the dance floor. He wanted the focus to be on Cassie as her pretty dress flared out with each turn, each dip. She moved like an angel. Light on her feet, she kept time perfectly, matching his footwork with her own. As the music built in intensity, Luke's feet moved effortlessly across the floor. His ears perked as the last stanza drew near. *This is it.* He gave Cassie the nod that told her this was the time for their special move. Her bright smile told him she was ready.

When the last notes sounded, he slid on one knee, thankful for the light dusting of sand on the floor, and the worn-in dance shoes on his feet. Without a hitch, he drew her down to sit on his thigh. The last beats of music gave him his cue. He lowered his head onto Cassie's lap and felt the light touch of her hand on his head.

Then he heard it.

The applause.

When he lifted his head, it was Cassie's eyes he sought.

They couldn't have danced it any better.

Chapter 14

As soon as Luke opened his eyes the next morning, he laughed out loud. He and Cassie won first prize in the country dance category last night! He still had trouble believing it. They'd managed to impress not only each other but Chet and Conrad as well. He could still see the surprise on Conrad's face after he and Cassie accepted their prize. And Chet, well, he couldn't stop shaking Luke's hand. A whisper of a new reality began to emerge in Luke's mind. Could he and Cassie have a life together? It would be a future very different than the one he'd imagined for himself.

Luke's phone vibrated on the nightstand, interrupting his daydreaming. He rolled over, picked up the phone, and saw the smile on his face reflected in the mirror across the room.

Russ Hunter's name illuminated the screen. "Hey, Uncle Russ, good morning."

"Luke?"

The panic in his uncle's voice had the hairs on the back of Luke's neck standing up.

"I've been trying to call for the last two hours."

This can't be good. Luke sat up and rubbed his eyes. The clock on the nightstand read *five minutes after seven.* "Yeah, sorry, I set the phone on silent before crashing last night. "What's going on?"

"We've got a fire. At the clinic!"

Luke bolted from the bed and crossed the room. "A fire?" He swung open the closet door. Using more force than needed, Luke winced as it banged hard against the wall before coming to a stop. "I'm on my way." He grabbed a pair of jeans and the first shirt he spotted.

Twenty minutes later, Luke eased into the parking lot crammed with fire trucks. A cold sweat broke out on his forehead as he watched the suited firemen at work. He didn't see any flames, but black smoke curled skyward from behind the clinic. *Oh no.* His mind raced and then settled on a sickening thought. He'd turned on the space heaters before heading to the wedding last night. His stomach lurched.

Uncle Russ ran toward the Jeep. His jacket flapped in the wind. The panic swimming in his eyes had Luke running in overdrive. What is he trying to tell me? His uncle was mumbling something, but with the window rolled up, Luke couldn't make out what he was trying to tell him. Luke threw the Jeep into park, cut the engine, and grabbed his jacket.

"What happened?" Luke asked, silently praying his actions weren't the cause of the damage.

His uncle waved an unsteady arm, directing him toward the undamaged side of the building. "This way."

Luke followed Russ away from the men at work to find a crumbling mess of what used to be a good section of the clinic's back wall. He scanned the area to the roof and found smoldering wood and shingles.

Uncle Russ dropped his head into his hands.

"Why now?"

Luke slipped an arm around him and pulled him close. It'd be better for him to come clean now before his uncle heard it from the professionals. "This is all my fault." Prickles of guilt rode up Luke's back. After the dance competition last night and their win, he and Cassie enjoyed an evening of celebration. It clouded his responsibilities to the clinic. It never occurred to him to check on the space heaters after seeing Cassie home. He should have.

Russ peered up at him through red-rimmed eyes. Disbelief washed over his face. He shook his head, already denying Luke's involvement in the disaster. "What do you mean?"

Luke saw the fire chief heading in their direction. Good. He couldn't wait to confess. If this was his doing, he wanted to take responsibility.

"I think I know what happened here," Luke blurted out the words as the officer approached. He raked a hand through his hair. What was he thinking when he'd set up a couple of worn-out space heaters to help speed up the dry time of the new interior wall? He should've known better. The least he could have done was check on the heaters before going home or ask someone else to do it. He'd done none of it. Not a single thing. Instead, he assumed his idea was sound and it would all work out perfectly like a naïve kid on his first big job.

Chief Reynolds gave Luke a serious look. "And you are?"

Luke's gaze fell to the badge on the chief's coat. He read the words encircling the emblem *Courage, Valor, Honor, Dedication, Service*. He sighed as the weight of his irresponsibility pressed on him.

"I'm Russ's nephew. My name is Luke Hunter. I'm a vet here at the clinic. I'm quite certain I know what happened here since I'm responsible." Even the words tasted sour on his tongue. So thorough and conscientious at work, he now stood before the chief as a total failure.

"What you're telling me, Dr. Hunter, is that you had a part in the brush fire a couple of houses over?"

Luke straightened up his shoulders. *Brush fire?* "Ah, no. I assumed it was caused by the space heaters I'd turned on last night."

Uncle Russ patted Luke's back. "I had Tom down at Meyer's Electric add a couple of auto-safety switches on those units in case they'd overheat."

Luke released a pent-up breath. "You did?"

After answering a call from one of the crew, the chief turned back to Luke. "We traced the damage to your building to a brush fire that got away from your neighbors. Mr. and Mrs. Esser are standing right over there and would like a word with you."

Luke bent over, resting his hands on his thighs, sucking in big breaths. His legs felt like rubber. "Thank you, God."

"You're not at fault here," Reynolds said. You'll have some repair work, but the Essers have already called their insurance agent."

"Thank you," Uncle Russ said.

The relief Luke heard in his uncle's voice did little to console him. Maybe he hadn't been responsible, but this situation had humbled him. He was still guilty of irresponsibility. Taking over at the helm of the business, with a flaw like his, did not go hand-in-hand.

This whole experience proved how much he was like his father. So, pursuing the job with PetsAmerica was the right move after all.

Uncle Russ slipped a Green Bay Packer cap on his head and then zipped up his coat. "Now that the worst is over, it doesn't look all that bad. It wasn't a sound wall, to begin with."

Despite it all, Luke's lips broke into a chuckle. *Always the optimist.* "I'll get right on it and get in touch with our insurance company…if you'd like." He wasn't sure if his uncle wanted him near the place anymore.

Uncle Russ tilted his head. "I'd appreciate that. See if he can come over this afternoon."

The vice-like grip around Luke's heart loosened. He turned to the man he respected and admired and hugged him, wishing now more than ever he was more like him. "We'll get through this."

"You bet we will," his uncle said, patting Luke's back with both hands.

As the fire department gathered up their gear and left the premises, the rattling of a diesel engine caught Luke's attention. Conrad's truck pealed into the parking lot and screeched to a stop. He and Chet jumped out of the vehicle and walked toward them.

"We came over as soon as we heard," Conrad said. Chet gave Luke a nod.

"I…what…" Luke couldn't process what was happening here. How did they find out about the fire when he had just found out himself? "How did you know?"

"I bought a scanner a couple of years back, so I'd know what's going on in my community. I'm also part of a volunteer emergency group in the village. When I heard about the fire here at the clinic, I got a hold of Chet," Conrad explained.

Luke directed his attention to yesterday's groom. "Aren't you supposed to be on your honeymoon?"

"We leave tomorrow. Andrea's home packing for both of us, so I'm sticking right here."

Uncle Russ turned to the men. "Listen, guys, thanks so much for wanting to help, but the insurance companies are headed over this way this afternoon. We can't touch a thing."

Conrad withdrew a notepad and pencil from his back pocket. "I'd like to take a look at the damages, so I know what equipment to bring. I won't disturb anything. As soon as you get the okay, our crews will get this place cleaned up." Conrad's take-charge attitude had him heading toward the back of the clinic with Chet on his heels.

Luke turned to his uncle worried the cold weather would aggravate his arthritis. "Listen, why don't you head on home? I'll talk with the guys here, meet with Ned, and bring you up to speed tomorrow at the café."

Uncle Russ buried his fists in his jacket pockets. "Thanks, my boy. That sounds good." He gave the clinic a backward glance. A forlorn look clouded his eyes.

Luke imagined what was going through his uncle's mind right about now. Maybe he hadn't let him down, and this fire wasn't his fault, but he was still haunted by what could have happened had those safety switches never been installed. He was incapable. "We'll get her back up and running," he assured the older man.

Uncle Russ grimaced. "This clinic is like a friend, you know? Been with me since the start. Your Aunt

Isabella loved working the reception desk. She handed out warm welcomes as if every person walking through the door were family. She helped me in the examining rooms too. Her favorites were the new pups." He shook his head. "Those curtains…" His voice trailed off.

Luke stared back at the clinic, his mind rewinding time, sharing in the nostalgic view. "I know. She'd made them herself."

Russ blew his nose in a red handkerchief and then slipped it back into his pocket. "After God called her home, it was the clinic that held me up. The reason I got up every morning. It kept me going. I'd look at those curtains and tell myself, she was here."

Luke squeezed his uncle's shoulder. For the first time, he understood the path Uncle Russ had chosen in life. It wasn't about making a fortune. His years at the clinic had given him satisfaction and comfort that you wouldn't find on a resume. "I've got this, Uncle Russ. It'll be as good as new."

Had his uncle heard him? His heart ached now that he finally understood how much this place meant to him.

Russ forced a smile. "I know you will. See you later."

Chapter 15

Cassie registered the pained look on Luke's face the minute he and his uncle walked through the café on Monday morning. He usually stopped in, had a cup of coffee, and took one to go for his uncle. Today, Russ followed him inside. She lowered the pot of coffee, placing it on a trivet. "You two look as worn out as I've ever seen. What's going on?"

"You haven't heard?" The serious tone in Luke's voice both surprised and concerned her.

Luke hung their jackets on the coat rack and headed in the direction of his favorite stool at the counter. His uncle took the seat next to him. "Just coffee today, Cass. I don't think either one of us could eat a thing."

"You got it. But first, tell me what's going on." Cassie filled two cups of hot coffee and placed them in front of the men.

"We had a small fire at the clinic yesterday," Russ said.

Cassie drew in a sharp breath. "That sounds bad." Even though Luke told her they weren't hungry, she reached for a prepared platter under the counter filled with hot breakfast sandwiches and muffins. Food had a way of settling folks down. She hoped it would work some magic now.

Luke winced. "The back wall will need to be replaced and part of the roof. By some miracle, Conrad and Chet showed up."

News of her brother's quick response caused Cassie to smile. "The new scanner Lila told me about. It doesn't surprise me he showed up on the scene when he did."

"They're planning to do the cleanup." Russ unwrapped the foil from one of the sandwiches and took a bite of the hot ham and cheese.

Luke grabbed a croissant. "Conrad said he'd start as soon as the insurance companies give him the green light."

"Should be done within a week," Russ said between bites.

Cassie rolled her eyes. "Big brother in action. He loves to clean up a mess."

Russ tapped his forehead with his fingers. "We forgot about something. I'm not sure how we're going to fix this one."

Luke dropped the last bite of his sandwich in his mouth and then turned to face his uncle.

"The pet adoption event," Russ said.

Luke rubbed his chin, remembering Chet's request for Andrea's wedding present. "Let's postpone that until next month. That'll give us time to get the clinic painted after the repairs are done."

Russ frowned. "I'll be gone by then—living in Florida. You sure you want to run the event alone?"

Cassie refilled their coffees. "I can help Luke out after the café closes."

"We don't expect you to do that," Luke said. His cool tone implied something more than the fire had gone wrong over the weekend.

Russ turned to Luke. "You're leaving on Tuesday for your interview, right?"

"Not anymore I'm not."

Russ's eyes widened. "Are you planning to reschedule the interview?"

Brushing Luke's icy comment from a moment ago to the sidelines, Cassie's heart soared. So much had happened between them, especially at the wedding. The moment when everything had changed between them. *The kiss.* The wonderful, unexpected, amazing kiss!

Cassie hid a smile behind her fingers, recalling when she leaned in and kissed Luke back. Maybe, just maybe, she could open her heart to love again. Had her prince finally arrived? She leaned in, resting her chin on clasped hands, drawing closer to the conversation. She wanted to hear Luke's change of heart. She didn't want to miss a word.

"I'll leave first thing Wednesday morning and be back later that night." Luke drained his coffee and returned the cup to the saucer.

As fast as Cassie's heart had flown with the hope of new love, it burst into a thousand pieces and fluttered to the ground. So that was the reason for his coolness toward her. He must've regretted all that happened between them. It was obvious to her now that their relationship had meant nothing to him. Nothing at all. The sting of what could have been, but would never be, ground salt in an old wound.

Cassie turned from the conversation and stepped toward the kitchen. She didn't want Luke to see the disappointment on her face or the tears collecting in her eyes. She'd allowed herself to fall in love with a man who told her from the start that he wouldn't be staying.

Foolish girl.

As hard as it would be, Cassie knew what she'd have to do next.

Heartbreak was coming.

Chapter 16

It was just after eight o'clock on a typical morning when Luke's phone buzzed. Half-dressed, he slowed the razor against his skin and glanced at his phone. *Lila Hamilton.* Concern flooded in. Had their dog Chester taken a turn for the worse? A few weeks ago, Luke prescribed a holistic pain med, suspecting a pulled ligament. But where older canines were concerned, anything could happen.

Luke laid his razor on the sink's counter, wiped his face clean of shaving cream with a hand towel, and answered the call on the second ring. "Lila, good morning."

"Morning, Luke. Any chance you could stop by this morning to check on Chester? Having a 90 lb. dog and a toddler to tote, I don't have enough arms and hands to navigate it all."

Luke chuckled at Lila's early morning humor. He'd have to set aside the visit to the ranch and the ride he was planning on, but he'd grown to enjoy making house calls, a task he now considered a perk of the job. "You bet I can. I'll be there in thirty minutes if that works for you."

"Thanks, Luke. I was hoping you'd say that. I'll

see you then."

Ten minutes later, he was in the Jeep, heading over to the Hamiltons. He hoped the old dog was okay. You never knew what you were getting with the rescues. Typically, their histories were not available.

Lila was waiting at the door when Luke pulled into her driveway.

He grabbed his bag and jumped out of the vehicle.

"Good to see you, Luke. Come on in." Lila led him down the hall to the kitchen where he spotted Bobby working on fitting a round piece of cereal on his chubby finger. As soon as the little boy saw Luke enter the kitchen, his feet kicked against the footplate of his highchair like a drummer banging out a tune.

"Hey there little buddy," Luke placed his bag on the floor and grabbed Bobby's legs, working them back and forth. The little boy squealed with delight. Mashed-up cereal dribbled from his lips.

"He makes quite a mess of things, but Bobby loves his cereal."

Luke's smile widened. He was beginning to look so much like Conrad. "What a sight." Then he shifted his attention to the dog.

Chester was sprawled out on one of the popular oversized bean bags for canines. The dog had barely moved since Luke's arrival. *Not a good sign.* Luke studied his breathing and then reached for his bag. He pulled out his stethoscope and started his examination.

"Heart and lungs sound good. No cloudiness in his eyes." Luke moved his hands to Chester's hind quarters. He placed one hand on the joint and lifted the leg with his other hand. He moved first in a clockwise motion then counterclockwise. Chester pulled his leg away and whimpered.

"It's okay, boy. I'll take it easy." Luke had his suspicions about what was going on, but he needed Lila's help for the next step.

"Lila, I'd like you to walk Chester away from me and then toward me. I need to observe his gait. Come on boy, up you go."

"I'll have to grab his leash from the back porch. He doesn't like to walk much if he doesn't have to."

After watching Lila walk Chester, the dog immediately returned to his favorite spot in the kitchen followed by a moan. Luke softened his look in Lila's direction. "I suspect Chester is suffering from the same ailment as my uncle."

"Arthritis? In a dog?" Lila's hands landed on her hips.

Luke rose to his feet. "It's not uncommon for the larger breeds, and it can develop at any time. We can run a series of X-rays to be sure and start him on a daily medication to ease his discomfort. But I need to warn you, it'll make him drowsy, and he'll want to sleep more."

Lila returned the leash to the back porch, returning to the kitchen. "He already dozes most of the day."

Luke spotted the disappointment on her face. "There is an alternative. A natural remedy that's called glucosamine chondroitin. It might help. You'll need patience, it takes about four to six weeks to see improvement."

Lila drew a heavy breath. "We knew when we adopted Chester, we'd face this issue sooner rather than later. But when he looked up at us with those big brown eyes of his, we told each other we'd found our dog."

Luke smiled at the unselfish decision to bring the rescue home. "That's a beautiful story to any vet's ears. He's lucky to have you."

"We love him dearly. Whatever we need to do to make him comfortable we're willing to do. I like the sound of the natural route. Do you have it in stock?"

Luke's spirits lifted. He preferred the first line of treatment to fall in the alternative medicine camp first. "I'm glad to hear it. We always have a supply. Most of our older pets are benefitting from the daily dose."

"I'll have Conrad stop by on his way home from work and pick it up."

"The clinic is closed for painting today, but tell Conrad the door will be open, and he should come on in."

Lila moved across the kitchen to the full pot of coffee on the counter. "Can I offer you a cup? There is one more thing I'd like to talk with you about if you have a minute."

Luke glanced at his watch. If there were other concerns about Chester he might as well address those right now. "I have plenty of time and a cup of coffee would hit the spot. I didn't have a chance to stop in at Cassie's yet this morning."

Lila walked toward the counter and filled a couple of mugs. She handed one to Luke and then offered him a chair at the kitchen table. After refilling Bobby's sippy cup with fresh water, she dotted the toddler's mouth with a moist towelette and then sat across from Luke at the table.

"I'm glad you brought up the subject of Cassie. That's who I wanted to speak with you about."

Luke leaned in. If this was about Cassie, Lila had

his full attention.

"You may not know this, but Cassie suffered a pretty bad breakup in college. It left her devastated for almost a year."

Luke shook his head. "No, she never mentioned it. What happened?"

Lila shrugged. "Two very different people trying to make it work. She's quite the go-getter and Sam was the complete opposite. It ignited a spark, but after a while, he blamed her for never relaxing, and she blamed him for not getting enough done. Lots of fights. Lots of makeups. Lots of drama."

Luke remained silent unsure how to contribute to the conversation.

"They were together a couple of years when he told her he'd accidentally fallen in love with someone else. She never saw it coming. Cassie puts up a pretty tough front, but she hasn't dated since, despite our blind date efforts. You add what she learned about Andrea's first marriage, and you've got a girl with a whole lot of fear."

The truth stole Luke's breath for a minute. "I didn't know Andrea was married before. Bad ending?"

Lila refilled their cups. "Her first husband accepted a doctor's overseas program. Neither one of them expected the consequences to their marriage with that one decision."

Luke's stomach dropped. So, this was why Cassie made such a point over the plus-one issue.

"You may have noticed Conrad's overprotectiveness over his sister." Lila sipped from her mug as Luke finished the rest of his coffee.

Yeah, he'd noticed Conrad's watchful eye from the

start.

Lila's eyes darted across the room landing on Bobby and then Chester—anyone but him.

He braced himself. Whatever was coming next was big.

Lila's gaze turned downward. "I accidentally stumbled upon you and Cassie the night of the wedding."

Luke's jaw dropped. *Oh, no.*

Lila drew back. This wasn't easy for her.

"Yeah, I saw the kiss. Or should I say, kisses?"

This was exactly what he didn't want to happen. "I see."

"I know you have plans that keep you moving. As Cassie's sister-in-law, I just don't want to see her get hurt all over again. She's grounded here. What I mean to say is, her family is here, her brand-new business is here, her livelihood." Lila shook her head. "And she's never once mentioned ever wanting to leave Door County."

Luke dragged a hand across his jaw. Everything Lila had said was true. "You're right. She's made that clear. I hear the passion in her voice when she talks about home and all of you. On the ferry, she helped me remember how beautiful Door County is. And anyone can see she's a natural with the café. Then there's her family. I get it."

Lila's eyes softened. "I think you have a decision to make. It might be one of the biggest of your life."

Luke blew out an unsteady breath, searching for the answer in Lila's eyes. It took a lot of courage for her to bring this up today. "Thanks for having the guts to talk with me about this. I'm sure it wasn't easy."

Lila rose from her chair and collected the cups. "I care about you both."

Luke was reminded of the unbreakable thread that ran through the Hamilton family. He was grateful when the conversation returned to Chester's care.

A few minutes later, Luke settled back in the Jeep and returned Lila's wave goodbye. *She's right.* What was he thinking when he leaned in and kissed Cassie and accepted her kiss in return? Luke's stomach clenched. It didn't feel wrong at the time. The world never felt more right.

A short while later, Luke pulled up to the clinic. He expected the painting crew to arrive within the hour and was surprised to find several trucks already there. He found his uncle inside behind the reception desk, stacking up the plastic desk chairs. Country music from a beat-up radio on the counter played quietly in the background.

"Morning, Luke. Great day to get the painting done. The workers arrived over an hour ago. Said you wanted an early start. Thought you'd be here by now."

"I would've been, but Lila called and asked if I could take a look at Chester this morning."

Uncle Russ's bushy eyebrows rose. "Oh? What was that all about?"

Luke removed his jacket and hung it on the wrung. "Hind legs are locking up. He's got the early onset of arthritis."

"Chester and I are in the same boat. Maybe he should ride in the backseat down to Florida with me." Uncle Russ chuckled and Luke joined in.

Luke reached for the upper medicine cabinet and grabbed one of the joint inflammation bottles. "I suggested we start Chester on the glucosamine chondroitin tablet."

His uncle grinned. "I taught you well if that's your first line of defense, but don't expect to have that option if you land the PetsAmerica job. It's all about making a profit in those big outfits."

Luke handwrote a statement and dropped it in the bag along with the med. He wrote Conrad's name across the front with a big, black marker and secured the bag with a staple. "I'll know more after tomorrow."

"Yup. The big interview and my departure to the Sunshine State."

The smile on his uncle's face told Luke all he needed to know. This was the right move for him. "How does it feel to be heading out?"

His uncle beamed. "Believe it or not, I'm excited. I've spent a good many years here in this clinic. Good years. But this winter get-a-way almost feels like a reward."

Luke's spirits rose with his uncle's perspective. "Don't forget I plan to come down and visit as soon as I can."

His uncle chuckled, lightening the moment. "That doesn't surprise me. They say once you live in Florida everyone wants to visit. I'll be popular for the first time in my life."

Luke threw him an exaggerated look. "Part of that is a true statement, the other part not so much. Your customers love you like family and you know it."

Russ's grin widened. "The best feeling in the world, my boy. You planning lunch for this hungry crew?" Luke was reminded of his uncle's golden rule—always feed your help.

"I've got pizza ordered for noon, and I ordered coffee and croissant sandwiches after the job is done." That was all Luke was prepared to say. He didn't want to accidentally spoil the surprise he'd planned for him later.

"From the Perfect Cup?"

Luke hung his jacket on the rung. "Yup. I wanted to give Cassie the business."

"She's a keeper, that one. Sees the best part of you and all your potential. S'pose you're planning on letting that girl get away."

Luke stopped dead in his tracks. His uncle had attended the wedding. *Did he see the kiss too?*

"Don't give me that look. Everyone sees what's happening between you two young people. It's nothing new, but it is something special. Maybe you think that comes along more than once in a lifetime. I'm here to tell you that it doesn't."

Luke and his uncle had many conversations over the last couple of weeks. Mostly about the clinic's sale, and his expectations for the new job, but this? A lesson on love?

Struggling to find a response that would satisfy him, Luke was interrupted by the door swinging open. More painters strode into the room. Luke breathed a sigh of relief. He wasn't prepared to talk about Cassie. Slipping on a pair of painter's overhauls, he buttoned up the front and headed down the hall. "Looks like I'd better get busy or risk getting called out for not helping."

"Hmpf. Don't think this subject is closed. We're going to talk about this later."

That was not a conversation he'd look forward to

having, and with what he had planned for later, he hoped his uncle would forget all about it.

~

Later that afternoon, Cassie showed up wearing a Perfect Cup Café apron. With her hair tied up in a swinging ponytail, she looked adorable. He spotted the coffee, croissants, muffins, and a large fruit platter on the check-out counter. Party favors and decorations dotted the reception room. A sheet cake that read *Happy Retirement* sat next to plates, napkins, and forks.

Luke walked toward her, keeping his voice out of Uncle Russ's earshot. She was standing on top of a tall cardboard box, trying to hang an oversized paper bell from the ceiling. He let a whistle sing into the room. "Wow. You went all out."

"Don't be surprised. You asked me to deck the place out." Cassie twirled around on tiptoes, inadvertently shifting the box beneath her. It moved in one direction while she moved in another.

Luke lunged toward her, catching her in mid-air, breaking the fall. His heart banged out rapid-fire beats. What if he hadn't made it? He wrapped his arms around her thankful that didn't happen, and she was safe in his arms.

Cassie's cheeks flushed as she tried to catch her breath. She smiled up at him as Luke placed her feet back on solid ground.

"It looks like you could use a little help."

She handed him the bow. "I have a hard time asking for that, even when I need it."

"I'm beginning to find that out. That's why I came in here. Something told me you were in trouble."

"I'm glad your gut instincts were right, or I

would've landed on the floor right about now. It would have been more than embarrassing."

After securing the bell, Luke motioned to the back room. "I've got Uncle Russ in the last examining room lifting the blue tape off the walls now that everything's dry."

"Good. When did the painters leave?"

"Forty-five minutes ago, maybe an hour."

Cassie's smile widened, warming every inch of Luke's body. "Perfect. The guests are pulling up now. Can you keep your uncle occupied while I get everyone in position?"

"You got it. And Cass, maybe we can talk later?"

Her expression turned serious. "I was going to suggest the same thing."

"You were?" *Is it possible we're on the same page?*

Cassie bit her bottom lip, an unusual habit for her.

Now Luke wished he didn't have a direct line to his gut reactions.

Something was about to change.

Chapter 17

Luke fought to slow his steps as he walked alongside his uncle. His anticipation grew for the surprise party he'd planned in his honor. "Well, I'm glad we finally got everything back in order. That was a bigger job than I thought it would be."

Uncle Russ smiled. "Me too. Now I can leave for Florida knowing everything is in order."

Luke paused, allowing his uncle to enter the waiting room first.

"Surprise!" A roomful of Happy Paws clients cheered and clapped.

Uncle Russ rocked on his heels almost backing straight into Luke.

"Go on, this is for you." Luke gave his uncle a gentle nudge toward a roomful of guests. A sea of smiling faces beamed back at them.

Russ looked over his shoulder. "I don't believe this."

Luke stepped beside him and then pulled him close. He was already wiping the tears from the corners of his eyes.

"How did you manage this with everything going on?"

"Your rotary card file," Luke smirked, now grateful for the time he and Cassie spent searching through it. Inviting all of his uncle's clients in hopes of a good turnout for the party was Cassie's idea. By the looks of it, a good majority of grateful pet owners had shown up. Luke breathed a sigh of relief. *Exactly what we hoped for.*

He surveyed the room, marveling at the bang-up job Cassie did with the reception area. Red and yellow paper streamers and giant bells hung from the ceiling. Happy Retirement placards dotted the shiny new faux wood tables, and his uncle's favorite country music station played on the radio. Cassie had thought of it all.

Russ spotted the picture boards on the wall that showcased an admirable career with his beloved animals. "I can't believe my eyes. Is this your doing?"

Luke's eyes moved to Cassie. "Not mine alone. I couldn't have pulled it off without my right-hand man, or should I say, woman."

His uncle chuckled and mouthed a "thank you" in Cassie's direction.

"It was my pleasure." Cassie lit the candles on the iced marble cake. She headed toward Russ. The guests followed close behind her. "For he's a jolly good fellow…" the crowd broke out in song.

Hours later, after his uncle had gone and the party favors were packed away, Luke closed the door to the reception area and turned to Cassie. She placed the last of her decorations in a box.

"I think that's it," she said.

It was time Cassie knew the truth and the decision he'd made. His conversation with Lila earlier in the day weighed heavy on his heart.

"How about we watch the sunset tonight?" He hoped the setting sun would help create the perfect ambiance for his words to flow easier.

"I'd like that." Cassie followed Luke outside to an outdoor seating area he'd set up for their overflow customers. She took a seat in the glider.

He placed her jacket around her shoulders and sat beside her in a nearby chair. "You might need this in case it gets chilly."

She gave him the first warm smile of the day.

"What a great party. Thank you for helping me as much as you did. I couldn't have pulled it off without you."

Cassie started the back-and-forth motion of the glider with the tips of her toes. "It took both of us working together. I'll never forget the look on his face when he saw all the people in the waiting area."

Luke leaned forward, resting his arms on his thighs. "He and Cathy leave at first light. They're as excited as a couple of kids."

"You'll be doing the same thing tomorrow morning but in the opposite direction. Are you nervous about the interview?"

The tone in Cassie's voice threw him off course. It wasn't like her to be rude. Bold – yes. Assertive – definitely. But not rude. Something was wrong.

Cassie wore a stiff smile before she directed her gaze to the parking lot.

Luke shrugged, unable to get a fix on her mood. His enthusiasm for what he had to tell her was fizzling fast. Despite his inexperience and the blunders that may come along with his decision, he'd decided to stay and run the clinic. How would she react to his news?

Luke slipped one foot over the other. "Not really. The fact that it's in Green Bay helps."

She turned toward him, her face catching what was left of the setting sun. The shadow accentuated her high cheekbones.

"Green Bay? I thought the interview was in Minneapolis."

"The HR director was called down to handle a dispute at the Green Bay office. They thought it would be an easier commute for me to meet there."

"Obviously. Sounds like you're already hired. They're being more than accommodating."

Luke heard it again. The uncut version of the new truth she must believe now that the interview is near. He couldn't wait to tell her his change of heart.

"You may be right. I thought the face-to-face meeting was to land the job, but the follow-up call I got the other day sounded more like I'll be completing the new hire paperwork. It's hard to figure out. Schultz told me he was looking forward to the meeting as if the job hinged on it but now." Luke shrugged. "I'm not so sure it's that important."

Cassie pulled her coat around her as the sun dipped below the horizon. "Looks positive for you then."

Luke felt the smile spread across his face. "That it does, but I'm not sure I want to pursue it anymore." He waited for the good news to hit her and expected her surprise.

Cassie's eyes widened, but her smile was missing. Wasn't this what she wanted to hear? Luke stifled his disappointment. Maybe she didn't understand what he'd meant.

She shifted in her chair to face him. Her eyes

blazing. "What? Why not? This has been your dream for *how long*?"

Uncertain how to neutralize her response, Luke sat tongue-tied. Finally, he said, "Dreams change." He hoped it could be that simple, and she'd roll with his decision, but knowing Cassie as he did, she'd give him a run on his new train of thought.

Cassie rose from the chair. Her jacket fell off her shoulders to the floor. "Not that fast they don't. I've heard the excitement in your voice and saw the thrill in your eyes whenever you talked about all the opportunities this new job would bring. You told me yourself you were raised to keep reaching for the next great adventure."

The stern tone in Cassie's voice was hard to miss. Luke got to his feet. He'd better get a handle on what was happening here before it all spun out of control. "Cassie, wait a minute here. Let me…"

Cassie raised her hand. "Let you…what? Talk me into your sudden change of heart. No. You need to experience the life you planned for yourself. It's what you've been working for all these years. This opportunity is what you went to school for, studied for, and waited for. If you don't, you'll always wonder what if. Or even worse, one day decide it's what you've always wanted and leave."

The conversation Luke had with Lila echoed in his head. "That's not going to happen. We're not Andrea and her first husband."

Cassie threw him a hard look. "Don't make this harder than it has to be." She grabbed her purse and jacket and headed toward her car.

Luke's mind went blank as he followed her

through the parking lot. Too many words swirled in his head. He couldn't retrieve even one that would make the impact he needed right now. *This is going all wrong.* Desperation clawed at his throat. *Think, think, think.* "I don't want to go anywhere, not without you," he blurted.

She kept walking.

Luke felt the hammering of his heart. "Hold on."

Cassie opened her car door.

It was all happening too fast. Luke moved to place himself between her and the open door, but his reaction time was too slow. His mind and his body were not in sync.

She finally turned to face him, eyes to eyes, heart to heart. "Luke, my life is here. This is where I belong. It's home. Your life is waiting for you. At least dare to go after it because I won't let you settle for anything less. I care about you too much to let that happen."

Luke shook his head, denying what was happening here. This would be the end of them if he didn't fix it and fast. "Don't go, not like this." He knew it was a weak argument. His heart strained in his chest.

"For what? We both know what I said is true. Talking about it won't change anything."

Luke raised both hands. He was unarmed for this response from her. He thought they'd be locked in an embrace and planning a brand-new future together. "I don't want the job."

"Yes, you do." Her clipped tone silenced Luke's next protest.

He stood frozen unsure what to do next.

She slipped into the car, turned over the engine, and took off.

What just happened? As Cassie pulled into traffic, Luke retraced his steps back to the chair he'd occupied a moment ago. He expected a whole different outcome than this. He sat in the dark for a long time, listening to the sound of crickets as twilight settled in. A shadowy figure approached from the parking lot. He couldn't quite make out who it was.

His heart soared as he rose from the chair. "Cassie?" he called out. Then his shoulders slumped as he recognized who it was.

Conrad approached. "Luke? What are you doing sitting in the dark? And why are you calling out for my sister?"

Luke fell back into his seat. He might as well be honest with Conrad now. "Do you have a few minutes?"

Conrad shrugged. "For a friend? You bet I do. Just let me text Lila and let her know I'll be late. She sent me over here for a med for Chester." After the text, Conrad silenced his phone and slipped it into his pocket. He took a seat next to Luke. "What's going on?"

Luke let his head drop. "I blew it, that's what. I thought she'd love to hear what I had to say tonight, but she annihilated it all. I couldn't think fast enough. I didn't know what to do to stop it."

"Who are we talking about here?"

Luke met Conrad's gaze and found the question in his eyes that needed answering. He was tired of running from the truth about how he felt for his friend's sister. This was it, time to get real. "It's about Cassie."

Conrad chuckled and the knot in Luke's gut began to loosen. "That sounds like my little sister. She's always been a spitfire."

"Tsk. She was livid." Luke shook his head. "I didn't expect that."

Conrad raised a hand. "Okay, hold on. Let's back up here."

For the next several minutes, Luke filled Conrad in on the events of the evening. "I've been wanting to come clean about my feelings for Cass."

"Feelings, huh? Lila told me what she witnessed between you at the wedding."

Luke expected as much. Conrad was an honest man in his personal life and his business. It didn't surprise Luke that he'd have the same truthful relationship with his wife. Luke gave him a sideways glance and found Conrad grinning.

Conrad leaned back into the chair. "We saw this coming long before you realized it yourself."

"We?"

"Yeah. Chet and I."

Luke moaned. "Listen that's not what this is about. I'm in a real bind here. I told Cassie I didn't want the job at PetsAmerica. That I wanted to stay here and run the clinic."

Conrad's chuckle lightened the moment. "I'm glad to hear it and so will a lot of other folks. That's good news."

"That's what I thought." Luke heard the argumentative tone in his voice. *Get a grip.*

"Huh? Are you leaving something out here because that doesn't make any sense?"

"She ended it. Practically pushed me toward the job. Said I'll always wonder what I missed if I don't take it."

Conrad leaned in, pressing his forearms on his thighs. "Half the time I'm not sure I get Lila's perspective on things, but I've learned to give her the benefit of the doubt. Maybe Cassie has a point. She doesn't want you pining away for a life you gave up for her. When's your interview?"

Now Conrad wasn't making any sense. What did that matter anymore? Luke blew out an exhaustive breath. "In the morning, but I'm tempted to cancel."

"Don't."

Chapter 18

Cassie flipped the closed sign to open with a heavy sigh. As routine as it was, she loved this simple task every morning. Today though, it fell flat. Ending it with Luke last night was harder on her than she thought it would be. After a restless night's sleep, she hoped she'd awaken with regret and discover a reason to take it all back. She found none, but that didn't mean her heart wasn't breaking. Deep down, her truth barometer landed right where it ought to. She'd been right to end it. This way, he could reach all of his dreams and not be held back.

Life had taught her to be careful when the warning signs glared a different version of the truth. It wasn't like her to ignore those lessons. She wouldn't let what happened to Andrea happen to her. As much as it hurt, it was better this way. She'd be saving her heart from another disaster down the road. Cassie wished there was a reason for doubt over that truth, but there was none.

"Everything okay?" Zoey gave her a questioning look. "You're not your chipper self this morning." The young waitress buzzed the minivac across the surface of the counter picking up tiny crumbs in the little machine's wake.

Cassie's heart tugged as the words left her mouth. A big part of her had trouble believing it was true. She and Luke were over. "I ended it with Luke last night."

When Zoey's eyes widened and her mouth gaped, Cassie knew she'd surprised her.

Zoey switched off the machine. "But it was going so well. What happened?"

Cassie moved toward the kitchen. She had to keep the day moving along as normal as possible. It would be the only way she'd make it through the day. The sooner she accepted her new reality the better. "He told me he no longer wanted the PetsAmerica job."

Zoey threw up her hands. "Great. Excellent. Just what you wanted to hear."

Cassie tilted her head. "I knew that was a flat-out lie."

Zoey followed Cassie into the kitchen. "No, no, no you didn't."

Cassie pinned her long hair back into a neat bun at the nape of her neck. "The last thing I want is to repeat the lesson of a broken heart. I learned that once already the hard way."

"Why can't you believe Luke truly changed his mind about the job?"

"Because he's waited for this moment for so long. Prepared for it in vet school. This is the exact opportunity he hoped would happen. It was a mistake falling for him. I knew that deep down, but I let myself fall in love with him anyway."

Zoey moaned. "Oh, Cassie, my mother has always told me there's someone for everyone and that includes you."

Cassie's hands stilled. Zoey made a good point, but the truth Cassie believed far outweighed Zoey's argument. Luke didn't belong here. He was destined for a whole different path. As much as she didn't want it to be true, he would always need a bigger life.

The world she lived in would never be enough.

She would never be enough.

~

Luke adjusted the knot in his tie, fighting the discomfort of wearing a suit. He grimaced as he stretched his neck over the crisp collar. He tossed the ballpoint pen he'd been clenching in his fingers onto the table. It wasn't the suit. It was the unexpected conversation he'd had with Cassie last night that had him in this rotten frame of mind. He still had a hard time believing she ended it between them. No, on second thought, it didn't surprise him at all. It was totally Cassie—high energy, feisty, free-spirited Cassie. He'd made the entire trip this morning from Sister Bay to Green Bay in silence, allowing a new truth to settle in deep inside of him. They were over.

It wasn't sitting well.

Glancing at his watch, Luke noted the time. It was just after nine o'clock. He was seated in a spacious but sparsely furnished office at the PetsAmerica Green Bay location. Although he'd been looking forward to this meeting, his enthusiasm waned. That was also bothering him. Like Cassie had said last night, this was the opportunity he'd been waiting for, so why wasn't he pumped to be here?

Luke expected he'd meet with Mr. Schultz, the director of HR. Instead, he was looking across a well-used wooden desk and into the eyes of Ms. Candace

Williams who wore a pair of leopard-patterned cat-eye glasses.

"Just to bring you up to speed on how this will work this morning, Doctor…" She glanced at the paperwork on her desk and ran a purple-painted fingernail up to the top of the page, then stopped. "Hunter." She lifted her green eyes over the application and met his.

Luke tilted his head. *Is she asking for clarification?* "That's correct."

"I typically handle the interview side of the appointment. Mr. Schultz will step in with the contract and welcome you to the corporation."

Luke was ready to get the process rolling. "Okay, shoot," Luke replied, and the interview began.

After thirty minutes of questions and answers, Ms. Williams removed her glasses and rubbed her eyes.

"This will be a big change from what you're used to. You're coming from…" Another quick look at his paperwork.

"Happy Paws Veterinary Clinic in Sister Bay."

Luke stared at her with irritation. What was wrong with him this morning? His nerves were on edge ready to snap. "Yes, I imagine it will be."

"Client base?"

He frowned, unprepared to answer the question. When was the last time his uncle tallied up their patient totals? *Tax time?* "Is that important?"

Ms. Williams slid the pen she'd been holding behind her ear. "Only if you're averse to maintaining a quota."

"Quota? How would a quota factor into a veterinary practice? Not sure I understand how the two are related."

She pulled out a laminated chart from a desk drawer. Columns of numbers, some red, some green, some purple stood out like stop signs, demanding his attention.

"Ideally, we expect our vets to meet a daily quota of patients, one every fifteen minutes. There are big incentives for vets who can break that number, and some do try and succeed. The red column represents meeting quota, the green is fifty percent above quota, and the purple one hundred. It can get very competitive. We have a digital leaderboard for our vets to track their progress in comparison to the other vets in the corporation. Most of our doctors enjoy the challenge."

Luke did a quick tally of the number of patients he'd be expected to see in a day. It was way beyond what they handled. It sounded more like a sales position to him than a doctor of veterinary medicine. Yet, incentive compensation tempted him to ask the next question. "What kind of incentives are we talking about?"

Ms. Williams broke out in the first smile of the day. "Trips, Dr. Hunter. Hawaii, Puerto Rico, Vegas. Golf getaways in Arizona. Ski packages in Steamboat Springs, Colorado. How does that sound to you?

Luke's eyebrows rose. "Tempting."

She might as well have said *excellent* by the smile that passed her lips. "The program is very popular. By making your quota, you help Mr. Schultz rise in the ranks among his peers and competitors. He likes to reward those who serve him well."

A concern that Luke couldn't ignore began to blot out the positives. "Has there ever been a quality-of-care issue? If I push it or rush a patient out of the office to meet quota, what does that say about my bedside manner or the quality of care that I'm trained to provide?"

She shook her head. "We have plenty of vet techs for that. No sense wasting your valuable, educated time on bedside manner."

He must have had a blank look on his face but decided to keep his next comment on the tip of his tongue. Uncle Russ had made it clear the value of a hands-on doctor who'd go the extra mile when needed, even if that meant getting in the car and making a house call to do so. He thought of the visits he'd made to Chester and Lulu.

"I don't imagine there's room for house calls?"

She laughed. "Any other questions?"

"What is the company policy on alternative medicines? I recently had a patient struggling with early onset arthritis and prescribed glucosamine chondroitin."

Ms. Williams shifted in her chair. "I'm glad you asked that question. We do offer alternative meds in our stores, but we'd prefer your first line of defense would be to support our pharmaceutical partner. That's another impressive reward program. Vets with high prescription numbers earn bonus dollars which are loaded onto a credit card to spend at their discretion."

Luke drew a long breath. This was a lot to digest. Could he make this drastic switch? It was a whole new way of practicing vet medicine, but the payoff would be the financial reward. If he bought into this program and gave it his all, he'd be able to live the life he'd always dreamed of having.

From the look in her eyes, Ms. Williams must've

picked up on his indecision. "Listen. There's a learning curve when you first join the organization, but we see many of our new vets adjust rather quickly and end up creating a wonderful life for themselves. I see you're interested in the three-year relocation program."

"That's correct and a big reason why I'm here today."

Ms. Williams tilted her head. "By relocating every three years, your concern over bedside manner isn't really important, is it? You don't have to concern yourself about building relationships. You'll be building a handsome income and a comfortable life for yourself instead."

She's right. "You make a good point."

She poured him a glass of water from the pitcher and placed it in front of him. "I know this is a lot to take in. As long as you meet your quota, you'll fit right in."

Maybe she's right, and he should ignore his uncle's voice in his head. He pressed his lips together in a tight smile.

She handed him a thick manila envelope. "You'll find the salary and benefits package including the bonus reward program with our partner, Right Choice Pharmaceuticals inside. Give it a look over, and I'll let Mr. Schultz know you're ready to sign on. If you're lucky, he might even reveal the store location he'd like you to start at."

Luke felt the blood drain from his face. "You mean it might not be in Wisconsin?"

Ms. Williams removed her glasses and placed them in a desk drawer. "Not necessarily. We have over twelve hundred stores across the country."

Leave Wisconsin? The thought hit him square in the gut. He'd never see Cassie again.

She rose from the desk. "I'll let Mr. Schultz know we've completed the interview. You are ready for him, aren't you, Dr. Hunter?"

Am I? Luke shook away the indecision that was eating at him. "Yes, thank you."

Luke heard the click of her heels on the floor and the door close behind her. He sucked in a big gulp of air and tossed the thick packet onto the table. Its contents spilled across his side of the desk.

Luke got to his feet and walked over to a large bank of windows that overlooked the city. Not far off in the distance, pillars of industrial smoke billowed from skyscraper-shaped chimneys toward heavy grey clouds. A sliver of morning sun shot through the cloud cover and fell on Luke's face. He closed his eyes.

Lord, what is missing here? The faces of his friends and family fought their way through the shadows of his closed eyes. The relief he saw on Uncle Russ's face when he walked through the door of the clinic on his first day back. Charlie McPherson's awe with the birth of a new pup. Lila's smile when he stopped by on a house call for Chester. Chet's gratitude when he assured him, he'd come through with a puppy for his new bride. Cassie kneeling right next to him helping to deliver Lulu's puppies.

Wait a minute. The truth hit him as if he'd opened the door to driving rain. He wasn't like his father at all. He didn't run from responsibility in search of the next job, the next "great adventure". He *was* dependable. And this whole idea of making a quota for veterinary visits? *Who am I kidding?* He'd never fit into that framework.

His thoughts drifted over to the relaxed pace at Happy Paws and how it helped calm not only the pets but the owners as well. If he accepted this job, he'd never have the privilege of caring for an animal for their entire life. Ms. Williams's laughter rang in his ears. He could forget about house calls right along with alternative medicine therapy.

With his eyes still closed, a sense of renewal charged through him. A truth he could no longer deny rang loud in his ears. It wasn't his uncle's voice he heard. It was his own. *I love the clinic!* The patients. The community. He even loved the old plastic orange chairs in the examining rooms. And he loved Cassie.

Luke's eyes popped open. Peering at the very same landscape from a moment, he now viewed it with a brand-new perspective. It looked as changed as he was inside. Beautiful in fact. He'd never been more certain or more firm about what he wanted.

He had to get home.

Chapter 19

Soon after Luke began the drive home, the phone rang, and PetsAmerica was displayed on the screen. Luke answered and listened as Mr. Schultz, although would have preferred to meet him, was prepared to offer him the job.

"Mr. Schultz, I appreciate the offer, but I've decided I'm not a good fit for PetsAmerica." With those words, the burden of trying to be something he wasn't lifted from his shoulders.

With a curt goodbye, his almost-boss didn't waste any time hanging up. A smile spread across Luke's face. Contentment filled him as if satiated after a wonderful meal.

He drove back to Sister Bay faster than he should have. The trip to the interview had worn him down. This trip home was soothing him. He was on his way back to Cassie. A few flecks of November snow hit the windshield as he approached Door County. Thanksgiving was right around the corner. If he didn't mess this up, maybe he and Cassie would be spending the holiday together.

He drove up to the Perfect Cup café and parked. He glanced at the time on the Jeep's display panel. *Three fifteen.* The café was long closed, and he expected Cassie to be in the kitchen working on the cleanup. He was counting on her routine which meant Zoey had left for the day.

He walked up the sidewalk and then raised his arm to knock on the door. *Wait a minute.* His palms began to sweat, remembering their last encounter. *What if she turns me away?* He fought through the panic and knocked hard three times and then he waited.

Cassie swung open the door and stood in the doorway. Her eyes were wide. She wore an apron that was stained with coffee and a smudge of icing.

She never looked more beautiful. Luke's pulse raced.

Her mouth formed an, "oh". Maybe she suspected he'd be long gone by now. Who would blame her?

"Surprised to see me?" he gave her a tilt of his head. He hoped he didn't see the backside of the door in his face.

She wiped her hands on a dishtowel and raised her eyebrows. "You could say that. I thought you'd be well on your way to wherever you're headed by now."

He guessed correctly. A lazy smile formed on his face. "It's getting cold out here. May I come in?" All he needed was an opportunity to talk with her. He prayed silently that if she gave him one more chance he'd do it right this time. He knew the truth about himself now. There was no turning back.

She glanced at the clock on the wall behind her. "I only have a few minutes. I'm babysitting Bobby this afternoon."

That didn't surprise Luke after witnessing firsthand how much love she already felt for the little guy. If he hadn't blown it the first time, maybe he'd be part of the caretaking team today.

Cassie stepped aside.

Thank you, Lord. Luke walked in and closed the door behind him.

Country music filled the room from the jukebox, soothing Luke's raw nerves. When had Cassie started listening to the ballads?

"I had my interview today."

Her lips went pencil thin. "When do you start?"

"I don't."

Cassie's hand flew to her mouth. "You didn't get the job? I don't believe that. You're a gifted vet and have an unmeasured love for animals. How could they not hire you?"

"I didn't stay to find out." He noticed the slightest curve of her lips. "I listened to the presentation, but it didn't sit well. It wasn't until I was alone for a few minutes that the truth hit me just like the wave that hit our boat on the ferry ride to the island. Remember?"

Cassie's face changed. "I do remember but wait a minute. Do you mean to tell me you walked right out of the interview?" Now she was smiling, and Luke's tense shoulders gave way.

"Yup."

Her eyes lit up. "So what truth are you talking about?"

"That everything I hold dear is right here. The clinic, the patients, and the relationships. The kind of vet that I want to become, the life that I want more than anything else. But more important than all of that, is you. The only adventure I want is a shared life with you."

He forced himself not to reach for her as the tears pooled in her eyes.

"Oh, Luke, you have no idea how much I prayed to hear you say that."

Luke's heart beat out of his chest. *I thought I lost her.* He opened his arms, and she walked into them. He stroked her hair and softly lifted her chin so his eyes could capture hers.

"I love you, Cassie Hamilton."

When their lips met, he knew without a doubt he'd made the right decision. Life fell back into sync once again.

She pulled back, and Luke spotted a hint of mischief in her eyes.

"I guess I caught myself a cowboy."

Luke whispered in her ear, kissing the soft spot on her neck. "If loving country music and a good pair of boots counts, it looks that way."

She placed her hands on the side of his face and peered into his eyes. "I love you, Luke."

His lips almost met hers, if not for an interruption from a very familiar voice. "Well, it's about time." Conrad strolled into the room with Bobby in his arms.

Cassie broke from the embrace and stared at her big brother. "Oh, my goodness, I completely forgot you both were here."

"That doesn't surprise me looking at what I'm seeing right now." He steered his gaze over to Luke. "I was counting on that interview to seal up this deal, and I'm glad I placed my bet the way I did on this one."

Luke's eyes widened. "That's why you told me to go to the interview?"

Conrad lifted his chin. "That's right. I figured it

would become really clear once you faced life without Cassie. I can't believe how blind you two have been. You've been in love for how long already?"

Cassie giggled. "Oh, like you're some kind of expert on love. Hand over my godson this minute."

Conrad handed Bobby to Cassie and stuck out his hand in Luke's direction. "It looks like we have another seat filled at our Thanksgiving table. Welcome home, Luke."

Epilogue

One Year Later

Cassie slid the last tray of peanut butter dog biscuits into the oven. She glanced at Ruby who was snuggled on her bean bag in the corner. "What do you think, Ruby? Will Lucy like them?" Cassie bent to ruffle Ruby's ears. The pup tilted her head and stared up at her with big brown eyes, causing her to chuckle. She's probably wondering what all the fuss is about.

Placing the dirty dishes in the industrial sink, she started the water and added the soap. She expected Andrea within the hour and wanted a clean kitchen. The two-dozen biscuit order was Lucy's favorite and in honor of her one-year-old birthday party later this afternoon.

Cassie always included the recipe, but few customers used it. That's what made her pet bakery such a success. *Let Me Do The Baking And You The Enjoying* was her store's motto. She loved it so much that she had an art student paint it inside the bakery's walls.

Cassie had started Pretty Paws Pet Bakery a few months after she and Luke were married. It was on their honeymoon that the idea to add a pet bakery to the clinic blossomed. What started as an idea to merge their talents under one roof, ended up being a reality.

Selling the Perfect Cup Café to Zoey was easier than Cassie had imagined. Listening to her plans for its future made it easier for Cassie to say goodbye. With Zoey's aunt's support and a small investment in the diner, she expanded the menu to offer lunch. The bus tour stops also boosted sales enough for the café to withstand the down season.

Remembering their wedding day brought Cassie into a moment of gratitude. They'd chosen one of Door County's quaint country clubs near the water. They'd been blessed with one of those lazy, warm summer days last July. The day flew by as most weddings do, but one memory that would never fade was dancing barefoot with her husband, under the stars, long after the guests had gone home.

So much had changed over the last year. The wedding, the business, and now Conrad was a few weeks out from finishing their home on a lot a half-mile down the road from the clinic. They'd chosen a timber frame structure on an acre of land. Luke wanted enough room for a horse of his own one day, and Cassie wanted farmhouse decor. They both loved watching it progress and agreed it was the perfect location to walk to and from work every day. Soon they'd move in, and their life would take another step into their future.

This was the life Cassie had always dreamed of but feared she'd never have. Luke had broken through her fear of giving love a second chance with his revelation that life with her was the only adventure he'd ever need. Cassie's heart melted all over again when she remembered the conversation between them that changed their lives forever.

With the kitchen sparkly clean, she still had time before Andrea would arrive to pick up the biscuits, so she made her way over to the clinic. As she walked into the examining room, she smiled finding Luke on his hands and knees, his dog Blazer right behind him. Cassie giggled. "What are you two up to in here?"

"Ah," Luke moaned. "I dropped a screw on the floor. All I wanted to do was get this cabinet put together, so you could see it. It's the one you thought would look the best in this corner."

Cassie's heart softened. Though he was a gifted veterinarian, when he tried to be a handyman, it didn't always turn out so well. She loved him all the more for trying. "Here let me help. Two sets of eyes are better than one." Cassie pulled a mini-flashlight from her pocket and cast its light onto the floor.

"I didn't know you had one of those."

"It comes in handy when I need the perfect light. There it is." Cassie bent over and reached for the screw then dropped it in Luke's opened hand.

Luke grinned. "You'll always be my number one assistant."

"I'm counting on that." When Cassie stood up straight the room spun around her. She reached for a nearby table to stop the swirling in her head. "Ohhh."

Luke jumped to his feet and placed his hands on her sides to steady her. "Whoa there. Are you okay?"

Cassie leaned into his embrace and waited for the spell to pass. A wave of nausea was sure to follow. "Well, I wanted to tell you tonight over a special dinner, but I guess that's no longer an option."

Luke's face paled. "Tell me what? You're not *sick*, are you?"

She gazed into the eyes of the man she loved, reading the concern on his face. It touched her heart. "Sick? No. Pregnant with our first baby, yes."

Luke whooped and picked her up off the ground. "Answered prayers."

"What? You've been praying for us to get pregnant?"

Luke beamed a wide smile. "You bet I have, and I couldn't be happier." He twirled her around and then stopped himself. "Oh, I'm sorry. I shouldn't be doing that. You just had a dizzy spell." He placed her feet back on the floor as if she were a fragile vase.

Cassie giggled. "I'm not going to break, and the baby is well protected."

Luke's smile broadened. "Good thing Conrad's almost finished with the house. Looks like we're going to fill one of those bedrooms right away." He placed his hands on her tummy.

She lowered her hands and placed them on top of his. "We'll be able to hear the baby's heartbeat on the next visit."

It was another one of those moments that Cassie would always remember. The wonderment in her husband's eyes. The love that flowed from his hands to hers. The truth he now understood.

Luke was home.

The End

Don't miss Falling For Chet.

9 781959 788843